WHERE FIREFLIES TAKE FLIGHT

MANYA

Contents

About the Author   v

  1. Runways And Heartstrings   1

  2. The Takeoff Into Tomorrow   8

  3. Nightlife And New Ties   16

  4. Too Much, Too Soon   30

  5. The Breaking Point   42

  6. A Friend In The Storm   51

  7. A Secret Between Us   58

  8. Fireflies And First Kisses   71

  9. A Breath Away From Forever   83

10. Goodbyes And New Skies   92

11. At The Brink Of Us   103

12. The Parting Call   113

Epilogue   123

About The Author

Manya has built a career in the aviation industry, one that has taken her to new places, introduced her to people from all walks of life, and filled her life with stories waiting to be told. She always dreamed of becoming a writer, but it took many life experiences, moments of doubt, and countless attempts before she finally decided to start writing.

Apart from writing, Manya has a deep love for music and dance, finding creativity and connection in both. She also enjoys meeting new people and values the power of shared experiences. In her debut book, Where Fireflies Take Flight, Manya explores the essence of finding one's way through life's unpredictable paths and the unspoken bonds that keep us going. She believes that every ending holds the possibility of a new beginning, and this idea shines through in her writing.

You can reach the author on Instagram :
mamta_patel_the_lucky_clover

CHAPTER ONE

Runways and Heartstrings

The night was warm, and the sounds of distant traffic mixed with the occasional rustle of palm leaves outside our balcony. The city never really slept, but time seemed to slow down inside our apartment. The lights flickered softly on the walls, casting shifting shadows as we lounged on the couch, relaxing together after a long week.

"What are we drinking tonight, Miraha?" Nina asked me, stretching her legs over the coffee table.

"Gin and tonic," Ayushi replied without hesitation.

I leaned back, letting my head sink into the cushions. "I'm starving. Can we order something?"

"Of course. And snacks. And my cigarette," Ayushi added, tapping at her phone.

"Yes, it's already in the cart," I reassured her.

"That's why I love you," she grinned.

The three of us—Nina, Ayushi, and I—met two years ago in India. We had walked into the same interview, sat nervously in the same waiting room, and left as batchmates. Now, we lived together in Dubai, sharing a home and a bond that felt deeper than friendship. Even though we had different personalities, we had become family in every way that mattered.

Nina, the most sentimental among us, was tall, fair, and had a round face that made her look younger than she was. Nina scrolled through her phone, a small smile playing on her lips. She was in a serious relationship, the kind that had history built into it. She and her boyfriend had been together since they were kids. He worked in the navy, stationed far away, but he visited her every couple of months when his schedule allowed. They made a good pair; he adored her, always pampering her and making her feel special. I had met him once, and there was no doubt that Nina loved him too. But their love came with its share of fights. They could argue over the smallest things, but the anger never lasted long. No matter how heated things got, they always found their way back to each other. Love had its way of keeping them tied together.

Ayushi, on the other hand, was different. She carried herself with a quiet intensity, a serious expression often settling on her face. She was tall, her dusky skin glowing under the dim apartment lights. Beautiful in an effortless way. But when it came to relationships, her world was anything but effortless. She was involved with a captain from another airline, someone whose base was also in Dubai. That meant they had enough chances to meet—on off days, during layovers in different cities, finding stolen moments in between flights. But their relationship was messy, tangled in something unhealthy. It was toxic, even abusive at times.

I never understood why she stayed. Maybe she saw something in him that we couldn't. Maybe she was too deep in love to let go. I hated him for making her cry. Their breakups were more frequent than their good days, but somehow, she always went back. Her story was complicated, one that deserved its own time to be told. The sudden sound of her voice cut through the calm of the room. "Why are you on a layover with that bitch again? I told you I don't like you talking to her!" Ayushi's voice was sharp, her frustration spilling over as she paced across the floor with the phone pressed tightly to her ear.

"Oh, shut up... fuck you, Rohan," Ayushi snapped before disconnecting the call.

Nina and I exchanged a glance, nodding slightly. This was nothing new. It had become part of our routine, like background noise in our lives. Ayushi lit a cigarette, her fingers shaking slightly as she took a long drag. She was furious. She always was after talking to him. It had become predictable. She'd argue, she'd cry, and then she'd pick up the pieces of herself until the next call. Nina barely reacted anymore. She leaned back into the couch, arms crossed. "Leave him," she said, her voice edged with frustration as she shot Ayushi a disgusted look.

I gave her a quick side glance, silently telling her to drop it. Nina rolled her eyes at me, her expression clear. I don't care. With a sigh, she got up, walked over to Ayushi, and took the cigarette from her hand before sinking onto the couch next to her.

"I will. Soon," Ayushi muttered, rubbing her temples. "You've been saying that for six months," I said. "It's time, Ayu. He's not good for you." She groaned, throwing her head back against the cushions. "Love sucks! But I love him... Ugh, I hate myself." "I agree," Nina chimed in, her tone dry.

"It's not like that, guys... come on," I said, shaking my head. "Being in love is beautiful. It brings joy and happiness. It inspires you to become stronger, to be better. It gives you comfort and support. We just need to understand it when it comes to us."

The room fell silent. I glanced at Nina and Ayushi. They were both staring at me, their expressions unreadable. A wave of embarrassment crept over me. I quickly turned away, avoiding their eyes as I reached for my glass and poured myself a drink.

"Well, well... someone knows a lot about love. Let's hear it!" Ayushi teased, nudging Nina.

They both started giggling, their eyes twinkling with mischief.

"You girls are pathetic," I muttered, rolling my eyes. "Don't talk to me."

I grabbed a cushion and hugged it, pretending to sulk. "Where's the food? I'm starving."

"It'll come," Ayushi said, waving me off. "But first, tell us more about this love you were just talking about. We need something to discuss while we enjoy our drinks and dinner."

"Yes, think about it... We hardly know anything about your love story or even a heartbreak. Anything?" Nina prodded me with a playful look.

"Come on, tell us!" Both rushed towards me, anticipation lighting up their faces. "Some other day," I replied, trying to dodge the conversation.

"No, we have plenty of time; it's our off day. We have all the time to kill. Start, I want to hear it," Ayushi insisted, not ready to let it go.

"Okay, on one condition," I bargained, seeing their eagerness. "If the food we ordered arrives in ten minutes, I'll tell you. If not, I won't. Deal?"

After a brief pause, both nodded in agreement.

We sat in suspense, the minutes ticking by. Then, about four minutes later, the doorbell chimed. Nina sprung from her seat and dashed to the door. She returned with a large parcel in her hands and a triumphant smile.

"Tough luck, Miraha!" Ayushi declared, a grin spreading across her face.

They quickly set about opening the food, arranging plates and drinks, and setting up the room as if it were a stage for my story. I took a deep breath, feeling the weight of the moment settle over me. "Okay..." "Yayyy!" Nina clapped her hands like a child waiting for a bedtime story.

Ayushi leaned in, resting her chin on her palm, waiting for me to start.

I hesitated for a second before speaking. "Four years ago, when I first got the airline job in India, it was one of the happiest days of my life. Mom and I were over the moon. We had worked so hard for this, and when it finally happened, it felt unreal. But that joy didn't last long. Within a week, I had to pack up and leave for Delhi for training. After that, I was posted in Hyderabad. I had no idea how long it would take before I could get transferred back home."

I paused, the memory playing in my head like a movie. "That one week before I left was a blur. We spent it running around, shopping for clothes, meeting relatives, packing, and making sure everything was in place. But no matter how busy we were, there was this unspoken heaviness hanging in the air. We both knew what was coming. The day I had to leave arrived too soon."

I could still feel that morning in my bones: the nervous energy, the lump in my throat, and the way Mom kept checking my bags, as if making sure I wasn't really going anywhere. "We reached the airport, and as we stood at the entrance, I turned to look at her. She was trying to be strong, but I could see it in her eyes. The moment I hugged her, the dam broke. Tears streamed down her face, and I felt my chest tighten. I had promised myself I wouldn't cry, but the second I saw her like that, I couldn't hold it in."

I swallowed hard, the emotions creeping back even now. "I somehow managed to pull away, wiped my face, and turned toward the entrance. Every step felt heavier than the last. I wanted to look back, but I knew if I did, I might not be able to leave." I took another breath, shaking off the memory. "I walked in, my heart pounding. I was scared, but this was what I had worked for. There was no turning back now. I followed the signs inside the airport until I reached the airline counter."

I exhaled slowly, staring at the untouched drink in my hand.

"And that... was the moment everything changed."

CHAPTER TWO

The Takeoff into Tomorrow

The airport was alive with the usual morning crowd. Passengers moved through the terminal with suitcases in tow, families hugged tightly as they said their goodbyes, and announcements played steadily in the background. I had just finished checking in and was heading toward security, gripping my boarding pass like it was the most important thing I owned. My heart was racing with a mix of nerves and excitement.

As I reached the boarding area, I glanced at my ticket. Row 30, middle seat. I sighed. It wasn't ideal, but I was too shy to ask for a change. Instead, I found a seat near the gate and waited, watching the airline crew as they moved around with effortless grace.

Soon, the boarding announcement crackled through the speakers, and passengers began lining up. I stepped forward, my fingers tightening around my phone. As I entered the aircraft, I noticed the crew standing at the entrance, greeting everyone with warm smiles. Their uniforms were crisp, their presence calm and professional.

"Good morning," one of the flight attendants said, her voice cheerful yet composed.

I returned a polite smile and handed her my boarding pass. She took a quick glance before pointing toward the back. "You're in Row 30, Seat B—middle seat," she said, gesturing in the direction I needed to go.

"Thank you," I said softly, then followed the aisle toward my seat.

As I reached the 30th row, I noticed a girl about my age already seated by the window. She had long, dark hair, and her gaze was fixed outside, watching the ground crew move about below. Without a word, I slid into my seat, adjusting my bag under the front seat.

Boarding was taking longer than expected, so I decided to call my mom one last time. She picked up immediately, her voice heavy with emotions.

"I got my seat, Ma. All set to leave," I said, keeping my voice steady even though my throat felt tight.

"Take care, beta. Call me when you land," she said, trying to sound strong, but I could hear the tears she was holding back.

"I will," I promised.

She gave me her blessings, and I hung up, staring at my phone for a moment. I was about to put it away when I heard a voice beside me.

"Are you going for cabin crew training?"

I turned to see the girl at the window looking at me with curious eyes.

"Yes," I replied. "You too?"

A bright smile spread across her face. "Yes!"

I felt a sudden sense of relief, knowing I wasn't alone in this.

"Miraha," I said, introducing myself.

"Saumya," she replied.

I took a quick glance at her. Saumya was tall, with striking South Indian features: deep black eyes that held quiet confidence and naturally pouted lips that gave her a poised look. There was something effortless about her presence like she belonged wherever she was.

After our quick round of introductions, we noticed that boarding had wrapped up. The doors were secured, and the aircraft slowly pushed back from the gate. My heart skipped a beat as I realized we were really about to take off. I couldn't contain my excitement. This was my first flight ever.

As the crew took their positions for the safety demonstration, I sat up straight, my eyes fixed on their every move. They performed each step with practiced precision, pointing out the exits, demonstrating how to fasten the seatbelt, showing the emergency oxygen masks.

I was mesmerized as this was a glimpse into the life I was about to step into.

The entire flight from Mumbai to Delhi, I found myself watching them, observing the way they interacted with passengers, and the way they carried themselves. I barely noticed the passing time, my nerves settling slightly with the thought that Saumya and I were heading for the same training. No matter how independent we think we are, having someone beside us makes things easier. At that moment, knowing that Saumya was on this journey too gave me a sense of comfort.

As soon as we landed, my phone buzzed. A driver was already waiting for us. He had both of our details and had asked us to meet him at the arrival hall. We collected our bags and walked through the busy terminal, scanning the crowd until we spotted a man holding a sign with our names on it. The sight made me pause for a second. I had only seen this kind of thing in movies, and now here I was—experiencing it in real life.

He greeted us with a polite nod and helped us with our luggage before leading us outside to the waiting car. As we settled in for the ride to the hotel, Saumya turned to me.

"Would you be comfortable sharing a room with me?" she asked, her voice casual but warm. I nodded. "Yeah, I'm okay with it."

I agreed without hesitation. "I'm okay with that," I told Saumya, feeling genuinely comfortable with the idea. In the short time we'd spent together, she had shown herself to be kind and easygoing, which made the idea of sharing a room with her much better than being with a stranger.

We arrived at the hotel and checked in, receiving our room keys from a cheerful receptionist who wished us luck with our training. Our room was a dual-sharing setup, functional and cozy with two beds separated by a nightstand, each side mirroring the other. It didn't take long for Saumya and me to get comfortable with each other. We unpacked our belongings, assigning drawers and shelf space, and soon the room felt lived-in.

That night, as I lay in bed staring at the ceiling, excitement and nervousness swirled inside me. Tomorrow was the beginning of something entirely new. Morning arrived faster than I had expected. The alarm resounded and both of us were up in an instant, already feeling the adrenaline rush of our first day of training. We got ready well ahead of time, making sure we looked polished and professional. Downstairs, the hotel's breakfast area was filled with other trainees, all filled with the same energy. Saumya and I grabbed a quick meal, barely tasting the food as our minds raced about the day ahead.

By the time we stepped outside, the airline bus was already waiting. The ride to the training center felt surreal as our new reality was finally beginning. As we walked into the training facility, we were greeted with warm smiles. Each of us received a small welcome kit with cute little goodies from the airline, including notebooks, pens, and a handbook outlining our training schedule. Soon, our instructor arrived, a poised woman with a commanding yet approachable presence. She smiled at us before speaking.

"These next three months are going to be intense," she said. "But by the end of it, you will be transformed. You will be ready."

I exchanged a quick glance with Saumya. We were ready for whatever was coming next.

The next few weeks were a blur. From the moment we stepped into training, life revolved around classes, studying, and exams. Sleep became a luxury, and rest was something we could only dream about.

Every morning, we woke up before sunrise, dressed in crisp uniforms, and boarded the bus to the training center. The days were packed with safety procedures, emergency drills, aviation rules, first aid training, and endless modules on service excellence. By the time we returned to our hotel in the evening, exhaustion weighed us down, but there was no time to relax.

Dinner was usually a rushed affair, followed by long hours of studying. We pored over manuals, memorized safety protocols, and practiced emergency responses over and over again. Some nights, we tested each other with mock quizzes; other nights, we sat in silence, overwhelmed by the sheer volume of information we had to absorb.

Days turned into weeks, and we barely realized how much time had passed. The routine was relentless: class, study, exams, repeat. It felt like we were caught in an endless loop, where the only thing that mattered was clearing each assessment and moving on to the next.

Delhi was just outside our hotel doors, but we never got the chance to see it. The city was lively, but it was just the backdrop to our training. The most we saw of it was through the bus windows on our daily commute.

Then, after nearly two months of this non-stop grind, something changed. One by one, we began clearing our major exams. The hardest parts of the training were behind us. The relief was almost unreal; after weeks of pressure and stress, we could finally breathe.

That evening, we reached the hotel around 5 PM. For the first time in weeks, there was no rush to study or prepare for an exam. We threw ourselves onto our beds, turned on the TV, and ordered food. It felt strange to just sit back and do nothing, but at the same time, it was exactly what we needed.

As we lazily scrolled through channels, Saumya suddenly turned to me with a glint in her eyes. "Let's go out," she said. "We've been in Delhi for two months and haven't seen anything. Let's explore. Let's go clubbing."

I sat up, surprised. I had never stepped foot in a club before. The thought of loud music, flashing lights, and a packed dance floor felt foreign, but also exciting. "Are you serious?" I asked, unsure if she was joking.

She grinned. "Completely."

I hesitated for a moment, then shrugged. "Okay, let's do it."

Within minutes, we were digging through our bags, trying to find the perfect outfits. Neither of us had ever dressed up for a night out, so we had no idea what was considered "right" for a club. After some debating, I settled on blue denim jeans and an off-shoulder t-shirt. Saumya went for black denim with a red tube top. We looked at each other and burst into laughter. This was completely out of our comfort zone, but we were doing it anyway.

By 9 PM, we had booked a pre-paid cab. At exactly 9:30 PM, we pulled up outside Sahara Mall, a place our classmates had mentioned as one of the best spots for clubs. The neon signs glowed against the night sky, the bass from inside thumping loud enough to feel it in our chests.

I stepped out of the cab, taking in the scene around me. The night was young and I had no idea what to expect, but something told me this night was going to be unforgettable.

CHAPTER THREE

Nightlife and New Ties

The moment we stepped inside, a wave of flashing lights and heavy bass surrounded us. The air smelled of a mix of perfume, alcohol, and something else, maybe excitement, maybe something unfamiliar. The music pulsed through the floor beneath our feet.

Saumya and I glanced at each other, wide-eyed, feeling like two lost kids who had wandered into a world we didn't quite belong to. Everything felt new: the dimly lit space, the neon lights and the bartenders moving swiftly behind the counter. The club wasn't as packed as I had imagined, but that was probably because we had arrived early.

Scanning the room, we spotted an empty two-seater table tucked into a corner. It felt like the safest option, away from the crowd but close enough to take in everything happening around us. As we slipped into our seats, I let out a breath, trying to absorb my surroundings.

We waved down a waiter and placed our order, some drinks and sides to munch on. Neither of us had much experience with clubbing, but at that moment, it didn't matter. The music had a way of pulling us in, making us forget the nerves. Even seated, our bodies instinctively moved to the rhythm, our excitement slowly replacing our hesitation.

Time passed, and before we knew it, forty-five minutes had gone by. The club had started to fill up, and the atmosphere had shifted. The energy in the room was growing with more people, more movement, and more noise. I could feel the heat rising, a mix of bodies swaying under the changing lights. I noticed a few guys at the bar throwing glances our way. It wasn't subtle. They probably sensed we were new to this. Their stares made me uncomfortable, but I pretended not to notice. I was here to have a good time with Saumya, not for that.

Time passed, and the energy in the club shifted. The DJ transitioned into Bollywood hits, and as soon as the familiar beats of *Kala Chashma* filled the room, Saumya and I couldn't help but cheer. The nervousness from earlier had melted away, and now we were just two friends, singing along to every lyric, swaying in our seats, and soaking in the moment.

When Gallan Goodiyan started playing, we clapped along, laughing as we tried to match the upbeat rhythm. It felt good, free, fun, and completely different from the routine of training and exams we had been stuck in for months.

In the middle of our excitement, a waiter appeared at our table, holding a tray with two mocktails. We frowned, exchanging puzzled looks. "We didn't order these," Saumya said.

The waiter gave a polite smile and tilted his head toward a table to our right. "Compliments from them." Curious, we turned in the direction he pointed. At the table sat three guys and one girl, casually chatting and sipping their drinks. One of the guys caught our gaze and gave a small nod, lifting his glass slightly in acknowledgement.

Saumya and I looked at each other again, unsure of what to do. After a brief hesitation, we decided to accept the drinks and waved a quick thank you to them before turning back to our own space.

Neither of us thought much of it at the time. It was a club, after all; people sent drinks, and people socialized. That was normal, right? We didn't even consider the possibility of the drinks being spiked. We were too caught up in the moment, too distracted by the music and the thrill of the night.

Thinking back on it now, I can't believe how careless we were. What if something had happened? I was so stupid.

As the night went on, the music picked up, and so did the energy of the crowd. The bass thumped harder, the lights flashed in sync with the beat, and the club felt alive. Before we knew it, Saumya and I found ourselves on the dance floor moving with the rhythm.

I had never felt anything like this before. The feeling of complete freedom, the rush of party music, the weightlessness of just letting go. It was intoxicating in the best way. I wasn't thinking about training, about responsibilities, or about the early mornings ahead. In that moment, it was just me, the music, and the thrill of the night.

At some point, I noticed the group from earlier joining us on the dance floor, the same guys who had sent over the drinks. I didn't pay much attention at first, caught up in the beat, but after a few songs, I started to notice the way the group had shifted.

One of the guys had taken over the DJ console, controlling the music while the girl from their table sat at the bar, sipping her drink. She was now accompanied by another guy from their group, and from the way they leaned into each other, it was obvious they were together.

That left two guys still dancing with us. I glanced over at Saumya and quickly realized that one of them had taken a clear interest in her. And from the way she smiled, the way she swayed just a little closer to him, it was obvious the feeling was mutual.

I suddenly felt a little out of place. With no other choice, I found myself dancing with the guy who had stuck around with me. We both exchanged a look, an unspoken understanding that Saumya and her new friend wanted some time to themselves. Neither of us seemed particularly interested in each other, but at that moment, we were just two people caught in the same situation.

After a while, the heat of the dance floor became too much, and we decided to step away for a quick break. The music faded slightly as we moved toward a quieter corner near the restrooms, away from the flashing lights and pulsing bass.

As we caught our breath, the guys followed, taking the chance to introduce themselves.

The one who had been dancing with Saumya was Siddharth, "Call me Sid," he said with an easy grin. The DJ from their group was Gurvir, though he went by "Guru." The girl at the bar was Chhavi, and the guy sitting with her, clearly her boyfriend, was Chandan. The one who had been paired with me by default was Rajiv.

A quick round of small talk followed, but I wasn't paying much attention. My mind was elsewhere as I had just checked the time. It was getting late. I turned to Saumya and subtly pointed at my watch, signaling that we needed to leave soon. Our hotel had strict rules; girls had to be back by 11 PM, with no exceptions. If we missed the deadline, there would be consequences.

Before Saumya could say anything, Siddharth caught on. "I can drop you girls," he offered casually as if it were the most natural thing in the world.

I froze. I looked at Saumya, expecting her to read my expression and politely decline. To my shock, she didn't. Instead, she nodded, actually nodded, and agreed without hesitation. I felt my stomach twist.

How could she say yes so easily? We barely knew these guys. What if they weren't who they seemed? What if this was a setup? All kinds of worst-case scenarios flashed through my mind. My gut told me this was a bad idea. But I didn't say anything. I just stood there, feeling the unease settle deep in my chest.

I took a deep breath, pushing away my unease as we followed Sid and Rajiv to the parking lot. The night air was cooler now, a slight breeze carrying the distant hum of traffic. The moment we reached the car, I hesitated for a second before sliding into the backseat next to Saumya.

It was just the four of us—Sid, Rajiv, Saumya, and me. Somehow, that felt a little less intimidating. At least if anything went wrong, it wasn't a car full of strangers. A small, ridiculous thought crossed my mind—I could probably take on two guys if they tried anything. My brain had already mapped out escape routes and worst-case scenarios.

I was so caught up in my own paranoia that I barely noticed how quickly we reached our accommodation. Safe and sound.

As we stepped out of the car, a strange feeling washed over me. Guilt. Not once, but twice, I had doubted these guys, assumed the worst and prepared myself for something bad to happen. But nothing did. Maybe they weren't so bad after all.

We thanked them for the ride, and just as we were about to head inside, Sid spoke up.

"Hey, let's stay in touch," he said, casually but expectantly.

I glanced at Saumya, half-expecting her to handle the response. She was already pulling out her phone.

This time, I didn't overthink it. I shared my number without hesitation. Something about the night, about how things had turned out, made me feel comfortable enough to do so.

The following week passed in a blur of training and grooming classes. Saumya seemed preoccupied, her fingers constantly tapping on her phone, texting away. She never explicitly mentioned it, but it was obvious she was in touch with Sid. Her occasional grins and secretive giggles were a dead giveaway.

"We should go out this weekend," she said one evening, casually tossing the idea into the conversation. "Same club, same fun, maybe even meet the others again?"

I looked up from my notes. "Again?"

She shrugged, trying to sound indifferent, but I could see the spark in her eyes. She was practically bursting with excitement, but I felt the opposite. The thought of going back to the same club or anywhere, really, was the last thing on my mind. All I wanted was to lie in bed, eat, and repeat the cycle for the next few days.

Thursday night had drained all my energy. We had our aircraft visit, an important part of our training, and it had stretched late into the night, wrapping up at nearly 2 AM. By the time we returned to the hotel, we were beyond exhausted. The only silver lining was that we had three days off with no training, no classes, just uninterrupted rest.

The next morning, or rather, afternoon, we barely managed to pull ourselves out of bed. When I finally opened my eyes, the clock read 2 PM. The only reason we even got up was because our stomachs refused to let us sleep any longer.

After dragging ourselves to eat, I flopped back onto my bed, stretching out with a sigh of relief. I was all set to do nothing for the rest of the day.

That's when my phone buzzed.

I lazily reached for it, expecting some random notification, but when I saw the sender's name, I sat up.

It was Rajiv.

Hey!! How are you?? Coming tonight??

I blinked at the screen, rereading the message as if I had imagined it. I hadn't spoken to him since that night at the club, so why was he suddenly texting me? And *coming where?*

Confused, I looked over at Saumya, holding up my phone. "Look at this," I said, reading the message aloud.

She barely reacted. "Oh, nice," she said casually, glancing at me.

I frowned. "That's it? Nice?"

She smirked. "So... you're going, right?"

I gave her an are-you-serious look. "Are *you* going?"

Her face lit up. "Oh, absolutely."

I sighed, already sensing where this was headed.

"Oh, please, Miraha. For me," she pleaded, putting on those exaggerated puppy eyes, the kind she knew I couldn't ignore. "I really want to go."

I groaned, running a hand through my hair. I had been so sure I'd spend the night in bed, but here she was, guilt-tripping me into changing my plans.

After a long pause, I took a deep breath and exhaled. "Fine. I'll come."

Before she could celebrate, I held up a finger. "But *only* until 11 PM. No later."

Saumya clapped her hands together in victory. "Deal!"

Saumya looked happier than ever, whether it was because we were going out or because she'd get to see Sid again, I wasn't sure.

On the other hand, I was still trying to process why Rajiv had messaged me in the first place. I hadn't really spoken to him after that night, and we hadn't exchanged more than a few polite words back then. Why was he suddenly so eager for me to come?

After a moment of hesitation, I picked up my phone and replied:

Yes, will be joining you guys tonight :)

His response came almost immediately.

Will pick you girls up by 8:30. See you soon.

I sighed, locking my phone and tossing it onto the bed. There was no backing out now.

The rest of the evening passed in comfortable laziness. We stretched out in bed, watching TV, scrolling through our phones, and ordering food. I was secretly hoping the exhaustion from our training would catch up with Saumya and she'd want to cancel, but her excitement never wavered.

By 7:30, I finally dragged myself into the bathroom for a shower. Every part of me wanted to ditch the plan, crawl into bed, and sleep. But I had already committed, and I didn't want to be the reason Saumya's over-the-top enthusiasm took a hit.

By the time I was done getting ready, it was exactly 8:30. I glanced at Saumya, who was still in the middle of her last-minute outfit crisis.

She groaned from the washroom. "Ugh! These guys are already here!"

I looked at her reflection in the mirror as she struggled with her hair.

"Miraha, can you go out and keep them company? I'll be there in two minutes!" she called out, her voice slightly panicked.

"What?? No way I am doing that," I replied, my voice tinged with annoyance.

"Please..." Saumya's voice trailed from the bathroom, laced with desperation.

I was tempted to drag her out by her hair for putting me in this awkward position, but instead, I just grabbed my things. Taking a deep breath to steady my nerves, I walked outside, mentally preparing myself to face Sid and whoever else might be there.

As I stepped out, I saw Sid and a guy I remembered as Rajiv waiting by the car. I waved at them, and they waved back. Sid's gaze quickly scanned past me, obviously looking for Saumya. I couldn't help but notice the anticipation in his eyes.

"She'll be out in two minutes," I informed him, trying to sound casual.

Sid seemed slightly embarrassed by his obvious eagerness and offered a sheepish smile in return.

Turning my attention to Rajiv, I took the moment to really look at him. In the daylight, his features were clearer. He had an average build but a very sharp jawline, which I hadn't noticed before. It was different seeing him like this, away from the dim lights and loud music of the club.

Just then, Saumya burst out of the hotel, rushing towards us while calling out, "Sorry, sorry, sorry..." Her voice was a mix of breathlessness and apology.

We quickly piled into the car and set off. The drive to the club was quick, and before we knew it, we were walking into the familiar sound of music and chatter. The whole gang was already there: Chhavi, her boyfriend, and another guy whose name escaped me.

We were led to a table right at the center of the club, which looked distinctly more upscale than the others. It was set apart, with a VIP vibe that was hard to miss. The perks of being friends with the club owners were immediately apparent. The table was decked out with large sheeshas, an assortment of starters, and a variety of drinks waiting for us.

We settled in, ordering a round of mocktails while the conversation flowed around us. I learned that the guy whose name I couldn't initially remember was Guru. He was not just the owner of the club but also doubled as a part-time DJ there. His question about my favorite genre of music led to a lively discussion about different musical styles. I mentioned my love for hip hop, which seemed to intrigue him.

As the evening progressed, our interaction felt as though we were long-lost friends reuniting after years apart. Guru excused himself and headed to the DJ console, where he started spinning tracks. Initially, he played a series of Punjabi songs. While everyone else seemed to enjoy them, I found it a bit hard to connect with the music, not being very familiar with the language.

Perhaps noticing my hesitation, Guru soon switched up the playlist, dropping some hip hop tracks instead. He gave me a knowing look and gestured for me to join him on the dance floor. The change in music revitalized me, and I couldn't resist. I found myself moving towards the dance floor, caught up in the beats that I loved.

As I danced, I noticed Rajiv positioning himself nearby, almost like a personal bodyguard. It was confusing at first, but his presence was reassuring rather than overbearing. He moved with a grace that complimented his strong build, and soon we were dancing together—close, but comfortable. Initially hesitant, I found his demeanor reassuring, and as he led confidently, I let go of my reservations and enjoyed the moment.

The night flew by, filled with music and laughter, and soon it was time to head back. As we walked to the parking area, Rajiv struck up a conversation, casual but pointed.

"So, you have a holiday tomorrow, right?" he asked, his tone casual but curious.

I glanced at him, sensing there was more to the question. "Yeah, finally," I replied, stretching my arms slightly.

He nodded, then, after a brief pause, added, "I was thinking... maybe we could go shopping? There's a great place I know, and I could use some company."

The question caught me off guard. Shopping? With him?

I hesitated for a moment, but something about the way he asked made it seem easy and effortless like it wasn't a big deal.

"Okay," I said before I could overthink it. "Why not?"

Rajiv smiled, and for some reason, I felt something shift. As I got into the car, I realized that somewhere between dancing, conversation, and the ease of the night, I had agreed to see him again. And maybe, just maybe, this was the start of something I hadn't seen coming.

Too Much, Too Soon

The car ride back to the hotel felt different. I stared out the window, watching the city lights blur past, the cool night air filtering in through the slightly cracked window. The streets were alive, but inside the car, everything felt still, except for the thoughts racing through my mind.

Rajiv had asked me to go shopping with him.

It was a simple invitation, nothing dramatic, but it had caught me off guard. I wasn't sure why I had agreed so easily. Maybe it was curiosity, maybe it was the casual way he had asked, or maybe I just didn't want to overthink it.

As I exhaled softly, I realized something. I didn't know much about him. We had danced, exchanged a few words, and now, suddenly, I was spending my day off with him. The thought lingered, stirring a mix of excitement and uncertainty within me.

By the time we reached the hotel, I had pushed the overthinking aside.

Saumya and I changed into our nightclothes, ready to finally crash into bed when, out of nowhere, she jumped onto my bed, eyes wide with curiosity.

"So... you and Rajiv are meeting?" she blurted out, her expression filled with suspicion and excitement.

I rolled my eyes, pulling my blanket over me. "He just needed company for shopping, that's all."

Saumya wasn't convinced. "Sooo, that's *it*? Just shopping?"

"Yes!" I replied, keeping my face straight, refusing to give in to her teasing.

The next day, I got ready around 2:30 PM, making sure I wasn't late. As I stood in front of the mirror, adjusting my outfit, I could feel Saumya's eyes on me. She sat cross-legged on the bed, arms folded, giving me that look as if I was sneaking off to do something scandalous.

"What?" I asked, turning to face her.

She smirked. "Nothing. Just watching you commit a crime."

I shook my head. "It's not a crime to meet someone, Saumya."

"Uh-huh," she said, unconvinced.

At exactly 2:50, Rajiv arrived to pick me up. As I stepped out, I spotted him leaning against the car, looking completely different from how I'd seen him at the club. He wore fitted denim and a formal shirt, and for the first time, I noticed he had glasses. I had no idea he even had a vision problem. He looked... good. Very different from the party version of him.

I slid into the car, still unsure of what kind of shopping we were heading for. Maybe clothes? Maybe something casual? But the moment we arrived, I blinked in surprise.

We had pulled up to a grocery store.

What?!

I turned to him, confused. "This... this is where we're shopping?"

Rajiv nodded, oblivious to my shock.

Of all places, why would a guy bring a girl to a *grocery store* on their first meet-up? My mind had pictured a casual shopping spree, maybe something fun, but this? I was *way* overdressed for a grocery run.

I followed him inside, feeling ridiculously out of place. He walked ahead, glancing around like a lost puppy, scanning the aisles without a clue of what he needed.

After a few minutes, he turned to me, looking helpless. Without a word, he handed me a list, scribbled in neat handwriting as if someone else had prepared it for him.

That's when it hit me.

I didn't know anything about him. Who was he staying with? Did he have a girlfriend? What was his full name? And yet, here I was, picking out vegetables with him like we had known each other forever.

How had I ended up here?

I sighed, glancing at the grocery list in my hands. *Maybe I was the stupid one after all.*

It took us almost an hour to finish shopping. Rajiv wandered through the aisles like he was lost in a maze, and I found myself guiding him more than I had planned to. By the time we reached the checkout counter, his cart was full, and I had half a mind to tease him about how clueless he was.

He paid the bill, and we stepped out of the mart into the warm afternoon air. Just as I was about to say something about heading back, he turned to me with an easy smile.

"Let's eat something. My treat," he said.

To be honest, I was starving too. The only thing that had kept me distracted so far was the absurdity of the situation, but now that we were done, my stomach made its presence known.

I simply nodded.

We walked down the street until we reached a Haldiram's outlet at the end of the lane. The place was bustling with people, the familiar aroma of chaats and deep-fried delicacies filling the air. We found a corner seat, away from the main crowd, and placed our orders: Pav Bhaji for me, Chole Bhature for him.

I had always believed that people in Delhi were obsessed with chole. Maybe it was just a stereotype, but looking at Rajiv dig into his plate like it was the best thing he had eaten, I was starting to think there was some truth to it.

For a while, we ate in silence. I was too hungry to care about small talk. But then Rajiv spoke, breaking both the quiet and my focus on food.

"Thanks, Miraha. Really. I needed this help today," he said, pushing his plate aside slightly. "I barely know anything about groceries... I don't even know how half of the things on that list look like."

I paused mid-bite, chewing thoughtfully. His honesty made me curious. I had already guessed that he hadn't made that list himself; it had to be from someone else. Judging by how lost he had looked in the store, I was certain it had come from a woman.

Without thinking too much, I asked bluntly, "So, who asked you to get all this? Your mom?"

Rajiv chuckled, shaking his head. "No, no. My maid."

I raised an eyebrow. "Your maid?"

"Yeah," he nodded, wiping his hands. "I live alone here, and she needed the basics for cooking. So she wrote the list and forced me to go get everything."

I felt something inside me relax, though I wasn't sure why.

"Okay," I said simply, nodding as I went back to my food.

We lingered at the table a little longer, falling into easy conversation. It was one of those moments where time slipped away without either of us realizing it.

I learned that Rajiv was from Nashik, Maharashtra, and that he had moved to Delhi for work. He spoke about his hometown with a kind of fondness that only someone who had left could understand. When he mentioned he was single, I pretended not to notice the way my heart reacted to that information.

Somewhere between small talk and laughter, the hours melted away. By the time we finally got up from our seats, it was already 6 PM.

Rajiv drove me back to my hotel, the car ride quieter this time, but not in an awkward way, more like a comfortable silence. As we neared my place, he glanced at me and said, "You should come to the club tonight."

I looked at him, slightly surprised.

"And," he added, "why don't you and Saumya stay over this time? You always have to rush back because of the hotel's 11 PM limit."

I hesitated for a second. Staying over? That was new.

"I'll ask Saumya and let you know," I replied, keeping my voice neutral, though I could already feel the idea settling into my mind.

Once I reached the hotel, I told Saumya about Rajiv's invitation.

She barely took a second to think before responding. "Done! Let's do it."

A small part of me had expected her to hesitate, but of course, she didn't. Excitement gleamed in her eyes, whether it was because of the plan or the fact that I was the one making plans now, I wasn't sure.

We got ready, taking our time since we were leaving early for a change. By 8:30, we had booked a cab and were on our way. I found myself looking forward to the night in a way I hadn't before. It wasn't just about going out, it was about seeing him. The realization caught me off guard.

There was something about Rajiv that had started to settle in my mind. Maybe it was the way he talked, the way he was straightforward without trying too hard, or maybe it was just the easy way time passed with him. Whatever it was, I couldn't deny it anymore.

By the time we reached the club, it felt like we were stepping into a familiar rhythm. Meeting, eating, dancing. The routine was the same, but something in me had changed. I was waiting to see Rajiv. And that was unusual for me.

This time, Rajiv didn't just casually pull me onto the dance floor—he *asked* me. It felt different, like a formal invitation rather than an impulsive move. I liked that. I placed my hand in his, and we moved toward the center of the crowd. The music pulsed around us, but as we started dancing, it faded into the background. His hands found my waist, pulling me closer, and before I knew it, I could feel his warmth against me. His touch wasn't hesitant. It was sure, steady. His fingers traced over my back, his grip firm yet careful.

I didn't resist. I didn't step away. It felt... right. As if I had already made up my mind before realizing it. The moment intensified when I felt his breath near my neck. A soft warmth that sent a slow shiver down my spine. His lips brushed close, so close that for a second, I thought I was imagining it. Then, in a low voice, he whispered, *"You are mine."* My eyes widened. My breath hitched.

Before I could process his words, he tilted my chin slightly, and before I knew it, his lips were on mine. It was unexpected. It was bold. But I didn't pull away. For a moment, time stopped. The club, the music, the crowd, it all disappeared. I let myself sink into the kiss, into the way his hands held me, into the way I had wanted this without realizing it. There was a part of me that knew this moment could change things, but right now, I didn't care.

Then, reality crashed back in. I opened my eyes. The music was still loud, but the silence around us was louder. People were staring. I swallowed hard as my gaze darted around. Guru and the others sat at the table, watching us with amused expressions. But the one pair of eyes that made my stomach drop was Saumya's. She was staring right at me, her face unreadable.

Embarrassment flushed through me as I stepped back, trying to steady myself. Rajiv still held my waist, but the spell had been broken. I exhaled shakily, avoiding everyone's eyes as we made our way back to the table.

Guru let out a teasing sound, the kind that only made things worse. A slow smirk spread across his face, and I knew what was coming. Saumya, however, didn't say a word. She simply gestured toward the washroom, giving me a look that made it clear I needed to follow her. I took a deep breath and nodded, then turned on my heels and walked behind her.

Once inside the safety of the women's restroom, Saumya wasted no time. Her voice was low but fierce. "Are you out of your mind??"

I leaned against the sink, my heart still racing from the kiss. "What? I like him, what's wrong with that?"

Saumya's expression softened slightly, but her concern was palpable. "A healthy flirting is fine, girl! But don't get serious, he is bad news."

I scoffed, folding my arms defensively. "Yeah, right! Coming from you, who is flirting and giving wrong hints to Sid? Wow!"

She shook her head, her tone serious. "I had a clear talk with Sid. I told him I'm not interested in being his girlfriend. He understood and respected that. There's a boundary there. And look what Rajiv did just now. You've met him, what, three times? Once alone... and he claims you in front of everyone. This isn't right, Miraha. I care about you, that's why I'm saying be careful."

Her words stung, mostly because part of me knew she might be right. But the feeling of Rajiv's lips on mine was still too fresh, the memory too vivid. "I know what I'm doing, all right?" I shot back, more to convince myself than her.

Saumya sighed, her stance softening. "I just don't want you to get hurt. Things like this... they can escalate. Just think about it, okay?"

"I'll think about it," I murmured, meeting her eyes in the mirror. I was still fuming as I walked out of the washroom. Saumya's words stayed in my mind, planting doubts I didn't want to entertain. She had a point. Rajiv's actions tonight had been too much, too soon. But I didn't care.

I wanted to do what made me happy. And at that moment, Rajiv made me happy. I straightened my shoulders and made my way back to the table where the others were seated. The music was still loud, the lights flashing in a rhythmic haze. But as I got closer, something unexpected caught my eye.

A plate sat at my spot, and on it was a perfectly square brownie. Written in chocolate sauce across the plate were the words Congratulations. I froze, confused. My eyes darted toward the others. Before I could react, Rajiv got up and pulled me into a hug. "Surprise!" he said with a grin, as if we were celebrating something significant.

Guru, Chhavi, Rajiv, Sid, they were all clapping, laughing, acting like this was some kind of anniversary celebration. I smiled, pretending to go along with it, but deep down, my mind was racing.

What exactly were we celebrating?

I barely knew Rajiv, yet here we were with a symbolic dessert and a moment that felt much bigger than it should. My thoughts kept circling back to what Saumya had said. You've met him three times. And he just claimed you in front of everyone.

I forced a laugh, cutting a small piece of the brownie and taking a bite. The sweetness melted in my mouth, but the bitter taste of uncertainty lingered far longer. As the night stretched on, the club eventually began shutting down, but none of us were ready to leave. Since we had taken permission to stay out for the night, we decided to linger a little longer, settling in for a final round of hookah at our table. The smoke curled into the dimly lit air, mixing with the scent of alcohol and fading music.

Time blurred, conversations flowed, and before we knew it, the clock struck 2:30 AM. Finally, we decided to move out. The group shuffled toward the parking area, the cool night air hitting us as we stepped outside. It was quieter now, the streets nearly deserted except for a few scattered figures in the distance. The breeze carried a slight chill, making me wrap my arms around myself for warmth.

Just as I took a deep breath, ready to shake off my thoughts and move on with the night—

A gunshot echoed through the air.

The sharp crack of it cut through the silence, piercing, sudden, terrifying. I froze, my heart pounding in my chest. The world around me slowed. The conversations, the laughter, the casual movements, everything came to a halt in an instant. And then, the fear set in.

CHAPTER FIVE

The Breaking Point

The sound had come from directly behind me. Time seemed to slow as I turned, each movement laborious, like moving through water. My eyes widened in horror when I saw Rajiv standing there, a rifle in his hands. The barrel was still smoking as he lowered it from where he had fired the shot into the air.

A chilling laugh escaped him as he lifted the rifle again. Before I could react, he fired two more shots into the darkness above. The sound shattered the night, and his laughter, manic and unhinged, filled the air around us. My body was paralyzed with shock; my mind raced to understand what was unfolding before me.

I scanned the faces of our group, seeking some sort of explanation or reassurance. My gaze finally met Saumya's. Her expression was grave, her eyes wide with fear and disbelief. She nodded at me subtly, a gesture that spoke volumes. It was a silent acknowledgment of the mess we had found ourselves in because of my association with Rajiv.

As the reality of the situation sank in, a deep, unsettling fear took hold. What had I gotten myself into?

The next week held the promise of my graduation, a milestone I had been eagerly anticipating. Soon, I would be leaving Delhi, returning to Mumbai before moving to Hyderabad for my new job. The thought of leaving this chaos behind brought a bittersweet relief.

On the day of my departure, Rajiv and the rest of the gang came to see us off at the airport. The farewells were a mix of awkward and solemn. Despite everything, I found myself promising Rajiv I'd meet him again. The words felt hollow, but they slipped out, a reflex of politeness in the midst of confusion.

Despite the unsettling events that night, I found myself continuing my relationship with Rajiv. I didn't quite understand why I was still with him. His behavior soon began to change; he became possessive and demanding. Whenever I missed a call or couldn't dedicate time to him, he would become upset or verbally abusive. It was clear that I was in an unhealthy relationship, yet something inexplicable held me back from leaving him.

I kept seeing him whenever I had a layover in Delhi, even though each meeting left me more drained than the last. Over time, I realized that Rajiv wasn't just verbally harsh; he was physically intimidating as well.

As the days passed, the demands of my flights and the toxicity of our relationship began to wear me down. Balancing the hectic lifestyle of my job with the escalating abuse from Rajiv became unbearable. I knew I had to end it for the sake of my mental health and well-being.

Determined, I arrived at my hotel in Delhi one evening and made a decision. I needed to confront Rajiv, to express how deeply his actions were affecting me. With a heavy heart but a clear purpose, I booked a cab to his house.

He greeted me with unexpected warmth when I arrived. The first thing he did was apologize for his recent behavior. He tried to explain his actions by telling me how much he loved me and that his mood swings were a result of us not being together more often.

Rajiv had gone to the effort of cooking my favorite meal, which only added to the confusion swirling inside me. Should I really tell him why I was here? He seemed so caring, so attentive. As he moved around, serving the food with a smile, part of me melted. I still had feelings for him, that much was undeniable. But the harsh reality of our situation couldn't be ignored.

Sitting across from him at the table, I listened as he shared stories from his week, his challenges, his small victories. He spoke with such enthusiasm, such love. It made what I had to do even harder. But deep down, I knew if I didn't end things now, I would remain trapped in this cycle of emotional abuse.

I took a deep breath, steadying myself. "Rajiv, stop," I said, my voice firm.

He looked at me, confused by the sudden shift in my tone.

"I need to talk to you," I continued. "I know you love me, but this relationship is suffocating me. I've just started my career, and this... this isn't helping me grow. I need a break—"

Before I could even finish my sentence, I felt a sharp sting on my face. My mind blanked, and a second passed before I fully realized what had happened. I had been slapped. I stared at him, frozen in shock, my hand instinctively flying to my cheek, my skin burning from the impact. Before I could even react, another strike followed, harder this time. I lost my balance and dropped to the floor, clutching my face, my heartbeat pounding in my ears. Everything around me blurred, but the one thing that was crystal clear at that moment was this: I should have walked away sooner.

Rajiv grabbed my hand and dragged me toward his bedroom. My body stiffened with fear. I wanted to resist, but I felt powerless. As soon as we reached the room, he pushed me hard toward the bed. My breath caught in my throat when I saw him pull out the same rifle I had seen before. Tears rolled down my face. My hands trembled as I struggled to process what was happening. A deep fear settled inside me. Was this how my life was going to end?

Rajiv rushed toward me, holding the gun, and I let out a terrified scream. He looked straight into my eyes and spoke in a cold, steady voice. "Don't worry. This isn't for you. But if you leave me, I swear I will kill myself right now. Everyone will blame you for it."

I could barely breathe as he continued. "And as for you, you are not going anywhere. You are staying here with me forever."

He turned and started walking toward the door. My instincts kicked in, and I ran toward him, hoping to escape. But before I could reach the door, he shoved me back inside with such force that I lost my balance. I hit the floor hard, panic taking over as I scrambled to get up.

Rajiv stepped outside and slammed the door shut. A second later, I heard the lock click from the outside. I sat there frozen, my hands shaking. My chest tightened, and I struggled to catch my breath. This was the first time I truly understood what fear and helplessness felt like.

I wiped my face and quickly searched the room for my phone. If I could call the police or anyone who could help, I might have a chance to get out. But then I remembered. I had left my phone on the dining table where we were sitting earlier.

I sat on the floor and cried. I didn't know for how long. My body felt numb, my mind exhausted from the fear and helplessness. Over and over, I pleaded with Rajiv to open the door, but there was no response.

The clock ticked away, and before I knew it, it was already past 3 in the morning. My flight reporting was at noon, and I couldn't afford to miss it. But right now, that was the least of my worries. My life, my job, my sanity, everything felt like it was slipping out of my hands.

I took a deep breath, forcing my voice to be steady. "Rajiv, I'm sorry," I called out. "I misunderstood you. Please, can we talk? You know I love you. It was my mistake. Please open the door. I don't feel good... I think I might fall sick."

I waited, my heart pounding in my chest. For a few seconds, there was silence. Then, I heard footsteps approaching. The sound of the lock turning sent a strange mix of fear and relief through me.

The door creaked open, and Rajiv stood there, staring at me. His expression was unreadable. My body acted before my mind could catch up. I ran to him and hugged him tightly. It was all I could think of doing in that moment. "I'm so sorry," I whispered. "I didn't mean to make you worry."

He didn't say anything at first, just stood there, holding me. Then, in an instant, his fingers tightened in my hair, pulling my head back slightly so I was forced to look at him. His eyes searched mine, his face unreadable.

"Don't do that again," he said, his voice firm but low. "You are mine. Remember what I told you?" I swallowed hard, still trembling. "I mean it," he repeated. I nodded, tears still streaming down my face. "Okay," I whispered, my voice barely audible.

Rajiv held me tightly, his arms wrapped around me in a way that made it clear he wasn't ready to let go. Then, without warning, he kissed me.

A wave of discomfort rushed through me, but I didn't pull away. Fear gripped me tighter than his embrace. If I showed hesitation, if I acted uninterested, he might lock me up again. The thought sent a shiver down my spine.

I forced myself to stay calm and managed to whisper, "I was wrong. I should have understood your love better. I shouldn't have hurt you." My voice was steady, but inside, I felt sick.

To make my act more convincing, I placed my hand on my stomach and winced. "I think I need to eat something. I don't feel well," I said, hoping he would take the bait. He looked at me for a moment before finally loosening his grip. "Go freshen up," he said, nodding toward the washroom.

I rushed inside, locking the door behind me. My hands trembled as I splashed cold water on my face, trying to steady my breathing. I needed to get out of here. I needed to find a way to leave without making him suspicious.

When I came out, Rajiv was smiling, as if nothing had happened. He had already prepared a plate of food for me, setting it down on the table like we were just another normal couple sharing a meal.

I played along. I forced myself to eat, pretending to still feel sick so I could keep my distance. The act continued for hours, stretching until 7 in the morning. I could feel my body giving up, exhaustion weighing me down, but I couldn't let my guard down.

By 9 AM, Rajiv had finally fallen asleep next to me. I took a deep breath, knowing this was my chance. I gently shook him awake and said, "I have to leave now. My flight is in a few hours."

He groaned, reluctant to let me go. "Can't you stay a little longer?"

I knew I had to be careful with my response. "I promised you we would meet again next week," I said softly. "You trust me, right?"

Something in my tone reassured him. He sighed but finally agreed.

On our way to the hotel, he held my hand while driving. Every now and then, he glanced at me and apologized for raising his hand. I nodded, saying nothing, pretending I had already forgiven him. Twenty minutes later, we reached the hotel. As I unbuckled my seatbelt, he leaned over and hugged me.

"Take care," he said.

"You too," I replied, stepping out of the car.

The moment I stepped out of the car and saw my hotel, I felt an overwhelming sense of relief. There was nothing I wanted to see more than that entrance in front of me. I walked toward the doors, each step feeling lighter, yet my body still carried the weight of everything that had happened. The past few hours had been suffocating, terrifying, and had shaken me to my core. Just as I reached the hotel entrance, I turned back one last time. Rajiv was still in the car, watching me. He smiled, and out of habit, I forced myself to smile back. I knew this was the last time I would ever see him.

As I stepped inside, my breath felt shaky, my hands unsteady. My mind replayed everything I had just survived. The fear, the helplessness, the way my entire life had flashed before me in those moments when I thought I wouldn't make it out. I had been scared for my life. I had been scared for my parents, my future, and everything I had worked for.

But now, I was here. I was safe.

A Friend in the Storm

The moment I stepped into my hotel room, I felt my entire body weaken with exhaustion. The door clicked shut behind me, sealing me away from everything outside. My legs felt heavy, my mind foggy, and for a brief second, I just stood there with my eyes closed, trying to process that I was finally safe.

But before I could take another breath, a sharp voice broke through my daze.

"Where the hell were you?"

I opened my eyes to see Suhana, my roommate and colleague, standing in the middle of the room, arms crossed, her face filled with worry and frustration.

"You were gone the entire night!" she continued, her voice rising. "I called you so many times! You didn't pick up, and then your phone was off. Do you know how scared I was? Aren't you supposed to inform someone if you're staying out? I was *this close* to reporting you missing to the seniors!"

I didn't say a word. I just stood there, staring at her. My throat felt tight, my chest heavy.

Suhana snapped her fingers. "Hello? Are you going to say something? Where were you?"

That was all it took.

I rushed toward her and threw my arms around her, burying my face in her shoulder as the tears I had been holding back finally broke free. My body shook as sobs wracked through me. I had no words, no explanation—just an overwhelming flood of emotions I could no longer contain.

Suhana tensed for a second before she let out a sigh and wrapped her arms around me. She didn't ask any more questions, didn't push me to speak. She just held me, her hands rubbing my back gently as I cried uncontrollably.

Minutes passed, but I had no sense of time. My body felt cold, my hands were trembling, and I couldn't stop shaking. Suhana continued to hold me, whispering, "It's okay. You're here now. You're safe."

Slowly, the sobs turned into quiet sniffles. My breathing steadied, but I still felt drained, my body weak from everything I had just been through.

Suhana pulled away slightly and looked at me with concern. "You look like a disaster," she said softly, shaking her head. "We have time to talk. Go freshen up first."

I nodded, wiping my face with the back of my hand. Without another word, I grabbed my towel and headed toward the washroom, hoping that the water could wash away even a fraction of what I was feeling inside.

After letting the hot water of the shower wash over me for what felt like an eternity, I finally felt calm enough to step out. My eyes met Suhana's as I emerged from the bathroom; they were filled with concern but also a kind of quiet strength that I desperately needed. My eyes were still red and puffy from crying, a clear sign of the ordeal I had just experienced.

"Come, let's go for breakfast," Suhana suggested gently.

I nodded, though a sudden worry crossed my mind. "What about our flight? Don't we have to report soon?"

She gave me a surprised look. "The flight's canceled. Didn't you see the notification? There's heavy fog. No one's flying out right now." I realized then that I hadn't even thought to check my phone. It was dead, likely because I hadn't charged it in my rush.

Relieved, we headed down to the hotel's dining area. I ordered a hot cup of tea, and we found a quiet corner seat. The warmth of the tea felt comforting, and I took a small sip, feeling it revive me. It dawned on me that I hadn't eaten in over a day. As I nibbled on some food, the reality of everything that had transpired began to truly settle in.

After a few moments of silence, Suhana's gaze fixed on me, earnest and expectant. "What happened last night? Tell me everything."

Taking a deep breath, I began recounting the entire ordeal from the previous night. Suhana listened intently, her expression one of deep empathy. She reached out and took my hand, squeezing it reassuringly. It was moments like these that reminded me why the bonds formed in aviation, particularly among crew members, were so unique and strong. Even someone I had known only briefly could become a confidant and a source of incredible support.

As I talked, the hours seemed to pass by quickly. We continued sipping our tea, which gradually turned cold as we got lost in conversation. Finally, as the morning wore on, we decided it was time to head back to our room. We grabbed some pastries from the buffet on our way out, planning to continue our chat in the comfort of our room.

Once settled back in our beds, I continued sharing my story, unburdening every fear, every moment of terror I had experienced. Venting everything to Suhana helped lighten the weight I'd been carrying. Sharing my fears and hearing her reassuring words made me feel, for the first time in a long while, that everything might eventually be okay.

As time passed, I knew Rajiv would start calling me. The thought alone sent a wave of anxiety through me. I wasn't ready to hear his voice, to deal with his manipulations again. Without second-guessing, I switched off my phone.

To avoid worrying my mother, I called her first. "I'll be resting today, Ma. If you need anything, call me on Suhana's phone," I told her, trying to sound normal. She didn't question much and just told me to take care.

Suhana noticed my hesitation and placed a comforting hand on my arm. "You did the right thing," she said. "And if he calls my number, trust me, I'll give him a piece of my mind."

I let out a weak laugh. I was grateful for her presence. She didn't judge me, didn't make me feel stupid for everything I had been through. Instead, she listened, helped me see where I went wrong, and reassured me that I deserved better.

The rest of the day passed in the comfort of our little safe space. We ordered room service, indulged in food, and let ourselves get lost in meaningless gossip and endless conversations. For the first time in a while, I felt normal again, no heaviness, no overthinking, just the warmth of my friends and the ease of being in the moment.

Later that evening, my phone buzzed with an unexpected call. Saumya.

It had been a while since we last spoke, and seeing her name on my screen brought back a flood of memories. I picked up, and before I could even say hello, her excited voice filled my ears. "Miraha, I'm in Australia! Can you believe it? It finally happened!"

I sat up, feeling a rush of emotions. Saumya had always wanted to move, to start over in a place that felt like hers. And now, she had done it. "Oh my god, Saumya! That's amazing. How's it been? How are you feeling?"

She let out a small laugh. "Overwhelmed, but happy. It's weird, starting fresh, but I think this is what I needed. And Miraha... you'll be okay too, you know? Whatever's weighing on you, you'll get through it."

Her words settled deep inside me, like a quiet reassurance I didn't know I needed. Saumya had been the first friend I made on this journey, and now she was in a whole new world, carving a new path for herself.It made me believe, even just a little, that fresh starts were possible and that I wasn't as stuck as I felt. The next day, we left for Hyderabad. It felt like a reset, a chance to leave everything behind. But just when I thought I could move forward, Rajiv wasn't done.

That week alone, he called me dozens of times from different numbers. At first, I ignored it, but when the calls increased, sometimes reaching a hundred in a day, I felt a gnawing guilt. A small part of me wondered if I was being too harsh. But then I reminded myself of everything I had been through. I couldn't allow myself to fall back into that nightmare. Days turned into weeks. The calls didn't stop, but I refused to answer. I knew that if I picked up even once, he would find a way to pull me back in.

Months passed, and life slowly began to feel normal again.

Suhana and I stayed in touch, even when we were assigned different flights. We made it a habit to check in with each other, whether through long chats, quick voice notes, or calls in between layovers. Whenever we could, we swapped flights just so we could be on the same schedule, making the long hours of travel a little more bearable.

She had become more than just a colleague; she was family. She knew everything about me, just as I knew everything about her. During one of our conversations, I finally told her how Rajiv was still calling me back-to-back. She didn't hesitate for a second before making me promise that I would never speak to him again. "No matter what, Miraha. You owe yourself peace," she had said, her voice firm.

I took that promise seriously, and I never broke it.

As time passed, our bond grew even stronger. We shared everything—our fears, our dreams, and the little things that made our days better or worse. Suhana had started dating a guy named Sean, and through her, I felt like I knew him too. Sometimes, when I was on the phone with Suhana, he would suddenly shout in the background, "Miraha, enough now! Give me my girlfriend back!"

Suhana would roll her eyes and hush him, but I would shamelessly tease back, "Nope! She's mine now!" The three of us would laugh over it, and in those moments, I felt light. It was a feeling I hadn't had in a long time.

With every passing day, the weight of my past started to lift, and for the first time in a long while, I felt like I was finally moving forward.

CHAPTER SEVEN

A Secret Between Us

The weekend had finally arrived, and I couldn't have been more excited. Suhana, Sean, and I had planned to meet up for a night out. Given my love for dancing, we decided a nightclub would be the perfect venue. It was Friday night, the air was crisp and filled with the promise of fun and freedom.

Sean and Suhana arrived to pick me up right at 7 PM. As I climbed into the car, I leaned forward and gave Suhana a warm hug from behind, while Sean caught my eye in the rearview mirror and flashed a sarcastic smile. I teased him playfully, and our laughter filled the car, setting a light-hearted tone for the evening.

As we drove through the city lights, Sean mentioned that a few of his and Suhana's friends would be joining us. I nodded, scrolling through my phone, half-listening. The idea of meeting new people didn't bother me; I was in a good mood and ready for whatever the night might bring.

Soon, we arrived at the nightclub. The place was full of energy, and the music was pounding even from outside. Sean called one of his friends to find out where they were. "Where are you guys?" he asked, peering through the windshield.

As he spoke, Suhana pointed excitedly towards a group near a flashy red car. One of the guys standing there noticed us and waved back.Sean moved the car a bit closer, and I tried to get a better look at the group.

We parked and got out of the car, and as we approached, my gaze landed on one of the guys. My heart skipped a beat as the man was strikingly handsome. Tall, with a charismatic presence, he had a look that could easily make any heart race a little faster.

Suhana grinned and made the introductions as we reached them. "Miraha, meet Ayan Khan," she said. Ayan stepped forward, offering a hand with a smile that matched his confident stance. "Hi," he said, his voice smooth and welcoming.

"Miraha," I said, introducing myself as I placed my hand in his for a brief handshake.

Ayan held my gaze, and for a moment, it felt like time had slowed down. His eyes locked onto mine with an intensity that sent a jolt through me. My heart pounded so fast I could hear it in my ears. This feeling—this rush—was something new, something unfamiliar. It was nothing like what I had felt with Rajiv. It was something entirely different, something I couldn't yet name.

"Let's go inside. The others are waiting!" Suhana's voice pulled me out of my thoughts.

Sean took the lead, holding Suhana's hand as they made their way toward the entrance. Ayan and I followed behind them.

As I stepped toward the club, a strange heaviness settled over me. The loud music, the flashing lights, the energy of the crowd all brought back memories I had tried to bury. The last time I was in a club, things had taken a turn I never wanted to relive. My feet hesitated at the entrance, my body suddenly rigid with unease.

Suhana must have noticed because she turned back, concern flashing in her eyes. Without a word, she reached out her hand to me, silently telling me that I wasn't alone. I hesitated for just a second before taking her hand.

Sean, who had been watching quietly, nodded in encouragement. The small gesture made something in me ease up. I envied what Suhana and Sean had. Their relationship was built on understanding and effortless care. They balanced each other so well, and for a brief moment, I wondered if I would ever have something like that. Pushing the thoughts aside, I walked in with them.

The music pulsed through the club, the bass vibrating under my feet. The energy was electric, people dancing, laughing, and lost in their own world. At the bar, two guys were waiting, casually leaning against the counter, chatting. As soon as they spotted us, Sean waved at them.

We walked over, and he introduced me. "Miraha, meet Kabir and Raj." They both smiled, giving me a casual nod. "Hey," Kabir said, raising his glass in greeting. "Hi," I replied, offering a small smile. Suhana and I talked every day, so even though I had never met these guys in person before tonight, I already felt like I knew them. Their stories, their personalities—Suhana had told me everything over our endless chats.

Raj was a South Indian who worked in an IT firm. He had been childhood friends with Sean and Ayan, and their bond was unbreakable. Ayan came from a Muslim family and, as Suhana had mentioned before, was going through a recent breakup. A small part of me felt guilty for feeling happy about that, but I couldn't deny the way my heart reacted whenever I looked at him. I was love-struck, and it made no sense.

Kabir, on the other hand, was a choreographer and happened to be Suhana's neighbor. Their families were close, almost like extended family. When Suhana and Sean started dating, their friend groups had merged, and from then on, they were one big, inseparable gang.

Despite meeting them for the first time, the energy between all of us clicked instantly. The conversations flowed effortlessly, and the laughter was natural. It was refreshing, being in a space where I didn't have to force anything.

Suhana, as always, had her own charm. She was a VIP member at the club, and the moment the DJ spotted her, he gave her a nod and played a song just for her. She grinned and waved back at him.

"Let's go dance!" she said, grabbing my hand before I could protest. The music, the energy, the flashing lights, it was exactly what I needed. I let myself move to the beat, enjoying the moment for what it was. For the first time in a long while, I felt free. But no matter how much fun I was having, my eyes kept wandering toward Ayan.

I didn't know why I was behaving like this, why I felt drawn to him in a way I couldn't explain. This feeling was different, unexpected but exciting. And for the first time in a long time, I didn't want to fight it.

After hours of dancing and soaking in the energy of the club, we decided to extend the night with a late-night drive and food stop. The idea of ending the night on a relaxed note, away from the loud music and flashing lights, sounded perfect.

We drove out to a small roadside food joint along the highway. Though it was nothing fancy, the place was full of people, mostly young crowds like us, gathered in groups, chatting and enjoying the warm food under the dim streetlights. It had that comforting charm of late-night food spots, the kind where conversations flowed effortlessly and laughter carried through the air.

As we parked and stepped out, a waiter approached us with menus. It was already 1:30 in the morning, and while I was enjoying the company, I knew I had to leave soon. I turned to Sean and Suhana. "Guys, I think I should head home now. It's getting late," I said, rubbing my arms slightly as the cool night breeze brushed against my skin.

Sean nodded. "Yeah, we should wrap up soon." Before leaving, we all exchanged numbers. I tried to act casual, but my heart did a little flip when I saved *Ayan's* contact in my phone. I wasn't sure why, but having his number felt... significant.

As I moved toward the car with Sean and Suhana, Ayan suddenly walked up beside us. "Let's all go together to drop Miraha," he suggested casually. "We have time to kill anyway." Sean shrugged. "Sounds good." I glanced at Ayan, feeling a rush of warmth at his unexpected gesture. He didn't *have* to come along, but he wanted to.

We split into two cars, with Sean, Suhana, and I in one, while Ayan, Kabir, and Raj followed behind in the other. As we pulled onto the road, I stole a glance at the rearview mirror, catching a glimpse of Ayan's car trailing behind us. Something about that moment made me smile.

My house was just fifteen minutes away from the food joint. The drive back felt shorter than usual, maybe because my mind was still lingering on the night's events. As we pulled up near my building, I turned to the group and smiled.

"Good night, guys. Thanks for the great night!" I said, unbuckling my seatbelt.

"Anytime," Sean said, flashing a grin.

Suhana gave me a knowing look, and before I could react, she whispered, "Text me later."

I shook my head playfully, stepped out of the car, and waved goodbye to everyone. Ayan's car was still behind us. He rolled down his window, giving me a small nod before I turned and walked toward my building.

As soon as I stepped inside, I felt warmth spread through me. I was smiling from the inside out, and I knew exactly why: Ayan. Weeks passed, and our little group continued to meet regularly. Whether it was for movies, long drives, or just standing near my building talking for hours, our bond had grown stronger. There was a sense of ease in our friendship, an effortless connection that made every moment feel light and carefree.

Ayan and I, however, had something different. There was an undeniable spark between us. It wasn't something we openly talked about, but it was there, clear as day, and everyone in the group had noticed. The way we exchanged glances, the playful teasing, the healthy flirting; it all added to something unspoken, something that neither of us wanted to define just yet.

And then there were the chats. The group conversations were always active, filled with jokes and random discussions, but the ones I looked forward to the most were my chats with Ayan. We talked every day, and not once did it feel forced or dull. The conversations flowed, effortless and natural, as if we had known each other for years.

It was during one of these chats that he told me something that made my heart sink. "My family wants me to move to New York for car designing," he said. "It's something I've always wanted, and they're making it happen." I stared at my phone for a few seconds before typing back.

"Wow, that's amazing! You must be so excited!" I meant those words, I really did. Ayan was passionate about cars, and this was a huge opportunity for him.

The exact departure date wasn't set yet, but the thought of not having him around was saddening. Despite these feelings, I reminded myself that we weren't dating or committed. It was just a budding friendship, maybe a bit more, but nothing that gave me the right to feel disappointed about his opportunities. I was happy for him, truly, because his dreams were coming true.

After a grueling day flying the HYD-DEL-HYD sector, I was completely drained. This flight pattern was always hectic, packed with numerous service requests and barely a moment to catch my breath. It was already 6:30 PM, and all I could think about was getting home and collapsing into bed.

Just as I was on my way home, my phone rang. It was Sean. I could hear Suhana's voice in the background asking, "Where are you?" "On my way back home," I replied, the exhaustion evident in my voice. "Okay, go home and get ready. We're coming to pick you up; we're planning a long drive," Sean announced cheerfully.

"No way!!!" I protested, my voice a mixture of fatigue and disbelief. "I am very tired; you guys go ahead. I can't join today." But Suhana wouldn't take no for an answer. "Come on! I saw your schedule; you're off tomorrow! You are coming," she insisted.

"No, I'm not," I said, trying to stand firm. I rattled off a thousand excuses, trying to convince them, and maybe myself, that I really couldn't muster the energy for a night out. Despite my protests, Suhana's enthusiasm didn't wane. "You need this," she argued, but I wasn't having it. Eventually, I ended the call, hoping they would go without me.

Twenty minutes later, I reached home. As I stepped inside, the comfort of my own space felt like a sanctuary. Dropping my bag by the door, I kicked off my shoes and made a beeline for the sofa. The thought of heading out again was the last thing on my mind.

After taking a long shower, I was ready to slide into bed and finally rest. My body ached from the exhausting flight, and the thought of curling up under my blanket was the only thing I wanted. Just as I was about to lie down, my phone rang again. I knew it had to be Suhana and Sean, still determined to drag me out for the drive. I sighed, already deciding that I was going to ignore the call or maybe even switch my phone off. There was no way I was stepping out tonight. But then I looked at the screen.

Ayan calling.

My heart skipped a beat. We had met a handful of times by now, and we spoke almost every day through chat, but he had never called me before. I sat up instantly, my mind racing with curiosity. What made him call me now?

I took a deep breath, cleared my throat, and finally answered. "Hello, Miraha!" His voice was effortless, as if calling me were the most natural thing in the world. "Hi, Ayan! How are you?" I tried to sound casual, ignoring the nervous energy building inside me.

"Good, good," he said. "I actually called about today's plan. We're all going, and if you don't come, it won't be the same. It won't be fun without you. Please come." The moment he said it, I already knew I was saying yes.

I had been firm with everyone else about not going. If I suddenly agreed now, they would definitely get suspicious. But at that moment, I didn't care. There was something about the way Ayan was convincing me that made it impossible to refuse.

I hesitated for a second before replying, "I'd love to, but I'm really tired. I was hoping to just rest tonight." "Please come... for me."

That was it. Those three words made my heart melt. I knew I was going, and I knew I wanted to go. "Okay," I said softly, smiling to myself. "Great! We'll be there in less than fifteen minutes," Ayan said.

"Okay," I replied before hanging up. As I put my phone down, I couldn't help but shake my head and laugh. Just a few minutes ago, I was so sure I wouldn't step out tonight. But now, here I was, standing up, already thinking about what to wear.

In a flurry, I rummaged through my wardrobe trying to find something appropriate to wear for an impromptu night out. My clothes were all over the place as I rushed to get ready. I finally settled on a casual but stylish outfit when my phone rang. It was Suhana letting me know they had already arrived. I quickly grabbed my things, threw my bag over my shoulder, and ran down the stairs.

As I stepped outside, the gang was already waiting near the car. The moment they spotted me, they erupted in loud cheers and whistles, making a big deal out of absolutely nothing, or maybe something. It took me all of two seconds to realize what was happening.

They were teasing me and Ayan. I rolled my eyes, trying to suppress a smile as I made my way toward Sean and Suhana's car. As always, I slid into my usual spot next to them, expecting the rest of the group to take their usual places.

But then something unexpected happened. Ayan walked past his usual car, opened the door on my side, and slid in right next to me. A slow smirk spread across Suhana's face. "Okay, what's going on here?" she teased, nudging Sean, who was already grinning.

I felt my face grow warm, but I refused to let it show. I turned toward Ayan, raising an eyebrow. "Seriously?" I asked, trying to keep my voice casual. He leaned back, completely unfazed. "What? Change is good," he said with a slight smile.

Suhana gasped dramatically. "Oh, I love this." Sean laughed but didn't say much, clearly enjoying the scene playing out in front of him. I shook my head, biting my lip to keep from smiling too much. The car pulled out of the driveway, the music turned up, and we were on our way.

The car moved smoothly along the quiet roads as the city lights faded behind, replaced by open highways and patches of darkness lit by the occasional streetlight. The night air was cool and carried a refreshing breeze, making the drive peaceful and pleasant.

Ayan leaned in slightly and whispered, "Thank you for coming."

I turned to him, meeting his eyes for a moment before smiling back.

The drive was perfect, far from the chaos of the city, with music playing softly in the background and the cool air brushing against my skin. But what made it even better was Ayan sitting beside me. I couldn't believe I had almost missed this.

As we made our way back, I sank into my seat, letting the music and the passing scenery lull me into a comfortable haze. Just as I was getting lost in my thoughts, my phone buzzed with a message.

I glanced down at the screen. *Ayan.*

Confused, I looked at him. He simply raised his eyebrows and gestured toward my phone, urging me to check the message.

I unlocked it and read:

Will you come out with me alone tomorrow?

My heart flipped.

A rush of warmth spread through me, my ears turning red as a thousand butterflies took flight in my stomach. My fingers hovered over the keyboard for a second before

I finally typed back:

Ok.

A second later, another message popped up.

Do not share this with Suhana or anyone. Is it ok?

I bit my lip, trying to suppress the grin that was threatening to spread across my face. This was something different, our own little secret.

Without overthinking, I replied with a simple ??.

Ayan glanced at his phone, then at me, his lips curling into a knowing smirk. And just like that, something between us had shifted.

CHAPTER EIGHT

Fireflies and First Kisses

That night, I stood in front of my wardrobe, staring at my clothes, completely lost in thought. I wasn't overthinking it, I refused to overthink it. This was just a casual outing between friends. That's all. But if it was just that, then why was I spending so much time picking the perfect outfit? I wanted to look good, but not like I had tried too hard. Something simple, but nice. Something that felt me.

I sighed, running my fingers over a few options before pulling out a dress and holding it up against me. "Is this a date?" I whispered to myself. No. No way. We were just two friends hanging out. That's it.

I'm not his girlfriend. He hasn't even said anything. But then a tiny voice in my head whispered, What if he likes me too? The thought sent a wave of excitement rushing through me. My emotions were all over the place; one second I was convincing myself that this meant nothing, and the next I was wondering what it could mean. I had no idea how tomorrow would unfold, and that uncertainty kept me awake for hours. At some point, lost in my thoughts, I drifted off to sleep, still wondering what the next day would bring.

The morning sunlight came through my window, making the room feel warm and calm. I got dressed in my favorite outfit: blue jeans and a bright red top that felt both casual and stylish. I kept my makeup simple, added some lip balm, and left my hair loose around my shoulders. Looking in the mirror, I smiled to myself. Something about today felt special.

Just as I was giving myself one final look in the mirror, my phone buzzed. Ayan had arrived. I grabbed my purse, gave my hair one last brush, and hurried out.

There he was, waiting in his car right outside my building. As I approached, he stepped out and walked around to open the passenger door for me. He was dressed effortlessly in blue denim and a black shirt, accessorized minimally. He looked absolutely stunning, or as I thought to myself, What an eye candy!

"I thought you might like this," he said, handing me a single white rose as I sat down. I took the rose, feeling a mix of surprise and delight. "White roses! Not bad... How did you know I love white roses?" I asked, genuinely curious.

He flashed a knowing smile. "I know a lot about you, more than you think," he replied. His comment sent a warm blush across my cheeks, and I couldn't help but feel a flutter of excitement. "Where are we going?" I asked, eager to know what he had planned.

"Not far, but not nearby either," he answered cryptically. "A place with good food and ambiance."

As he shut the door and walked to the driver's side, I placed the white rose gently on my lap and took in its light scent. Every moment with him felt like starting a new chapter in a story I couldn't wait to keep reading.

He got in, started the car, and we drove away from the curb.

The car slowed as we approached a serene lakeside spot. The place had an old-school charm with open stalls lining the area, offering street food and refreshments. There were no designated seating areas, making it feel more like a drive-in experience.

Ayan parked near the edge of the lake, where the view was breathtaking. The still water reflected the twinkling city lights in the distance, and a gentle breeze carried the faint hum of conversations and the occasional sizzle from the food stalls. As he switched off the engine, he tapped a few buttons on the screen, and soon, the soft tune of Take My Breath Away from Top Gun filled the car.

My eyes widened in surprise. Again? Another one of my favorites?

I turned to look at him, trying to hide how impressed I was, but the smirk on his face told me he knew exactly what he was doing.

"You planned this, didn't you?" I teased.

He shrugged casually. "Maybe."

Ayan leaned back, his hands resting comfortably on the steering wheel. "So, do you want to step outside and sit by the lake, or should we just stay in here?"

I glanced at the open stalls and the people gathered around, but my gaze kept drifting back to the view ahead of us: the lake stretching endlessly under the night sky, the music playing softly in the background, and Ayan sitting right next to me.

"Let's stay in the car," I said. "The view is perfect from here."

He nodded, as if he had expected that answer.

We ordered refreshing mint coolers from one of the stalls, and as we waited, we slipped into easy conversation. Ayan was in a playful mood, cracking jokes and making me laugh more than I had in weeks. It felt effortless, natural, like we had known each other far longer than we actually had. Somewhere between the laughter and the comfortable silences, the conversation shifted. We started talking about our past.

Ayan already knew bits and pieces about my relationship with Rajiv since Suhana had shared some details with him, but tonight, I filled in the blanks. For the first time, I spoke about everything: the pain, the control, the fear. I expected to feel vulnerable, but instead, I felt lighter, as if saying it out loud was helping me finally leave it behind. Ayan listened intently, never interrupting, never judging. When I finished, he sighed and leaned back against his seat.

"You deserved better, Miraha," he said simply.

I nodded, offering him a small smile before asking, "What about you? What's your story?" He exhaled, running a hand through his hair. "It's not as bad as yours, but it wasn't easy either," he admitted.

He told me about his ex-girlfriend, how they met, how they fell in love, and how everything changed when her family found out. They had been happy, but when her parents learned about their relationship, things spiraled out of control. They pressured Ayan to marry her immediately. But he wasn't ready, he had dreams to chase, a future he wanted to build before settling down.

"I had no choice but to let her go," he said, staring out at the lake. His voice was calm, but there was something heavy in his words, a quiet sadness he wasn't letting fully show. For a few moments, we just sat there, letting the weight of our stories settle between us. There was no need for unnecessary words.

After sharing our stories, a quiet understanding grew between us. We both knew what it felt like to love and lose. As evening came, the sky turned shades of orange and purple, giving us an incredible sunset to admire. The beautiful view made our earlier conversation feel a little less heavy. Lost in the beauty of the sunset, I was startled when Ayan broke the silence. "I need to tell you something..." he began hesitantly. "You know that day when you were denying to come out for the long drive when Suhana and Sean called you?"

"Yes, what about it?" I asked, curious about where this was going.

Ayan took a deep breath, his gaze fixed on the horizon. "I was forced to call you that time. Because, as per the others, you would not deny if I asked you... And guess what? They were right. You actually came. I felt like the king of the world that day."

His confession surprised me, and a mix of emotions washed over me. "What! This is bad, now I'm embarrassed... But why would they think like that?"

"Because I like you!" he blurted out, then quickly added, "And they think the feelings are mutual between us... Is it?"

His words made my heart flutter, and I could feel my cheeks warming up from a blush. "I really do, Miraha... I really like you," Ayan continued earnestly, "and I would like to know more about you."

His admission caught me off guard, but in a good way. The sincerity in his voice made my heart race. "Me too," I replied softly.

We both smiled, the tension of the moment dissolving into the fading light. It felt like a new beginning was on the horizon, just as the sun set, leaving behind the promise of something wonderful.

We spent the rest of the evening talking about anything and everything, from our favorite movies to our future dreams. As the night went on, the stars filled the sky, and we sat together, sharing stories and laughing.

Ayan's presence had a way of making everything seem brighter, more hopeful. It was clear that what we were starting to build was something special.

After that day, meeting Ayan became a regular thing. At first, we met with the gang, keeping things as they were, laughing, joking, and hanging out like nothing had changed. But gradually, we started carving out time just for the two of us. On the surface, nothing drastic had shifted. But beneath it, something was definitely happening.

When we were alone, small, unspoken gestures began to fill the spaces between us, his fingers grazing mine as he handed me something, the way his knee would brush against mine when we sat next to each other, the lingering eye contact that neither of us dared to break too soon. There was this magnetic pull between us, something neither of us acknowledged out loud but felt with every glance, every touch, every moment of silence charged with unsaid words.

We wanted to feel closer to each other. And yet, we never crossed the line. At least, not yet.

I was certain about how much I was drawn to Ayan, but I never made the first move. What if I was wrong? What if I had misread things? The fear of stepping into something uncertain held me back.

Ayan, on the other hand, had moments where he came so close that I could feel his breath against my skin. Our faces would linger inches apart, neither of us daring to take that final step forward. It wasn't hesitation. It wasn't disinterest. It was fear, fear of history repeating itself, of stepping into something that could hurt just as much as our pasts had.

So we stayed in this undefined space, where we weren't dating, but we weren't just friends either. It was a secret we both silently agreed to keep. Many times, I thought about telling Suhana. There were moments when I wanted to spill everything, to talk about how Ayan made me feel, how different this connection was. But something held me back. Maybe I needed more time. Maybe I wanted to be sure of what *this* was before I put it into words. For now, I was content with what we had: the stolen moments, the lingering touches, the late-night conversations.

One night, Ayan and I managed to avoid meeting Suhana and the others. I told them I'd be back late from my flight and wouldn't be able to make it. Ayan had given some excuse of his own. In reality, we had made our own secret plan. There was a place he had been wanting to show me, somewhere he had never taken anyone before.

After my flight, I went home, freshened up, and changed. By now, the pressure to dress up and impress each other had faded. We had grown comfortable in each other's presence, to the point where we met in our regular clothes without worrying about how we looked.

Ayan arrived at my place right on time, and we set off. The drive was different from our usual ones. The roads were unfamiliar and quieter than the ones we usually took. We weren't heading toward our usual spots or places we had explored before. This was somewhere new.

I glanced at him a few times during the drive, curious but not questioning him just yet. After about twenty minutes, Ayan finally pulled over. I stepped out and looked around, confused.

The place felt isolated. There were no people around, just an open stretch of land overlooking the distant city skyline. From where we stood, I could see the city lights shimmering far away, but here, in this moment, it was just us. I turned toward Ayan, my brows furrowed. "What is this place? And why are we here?"

But before I could say anything else, I realized just how close he was. I had been expecting an answer, but instead, I found myself caught in the intensity of his gaze. There was something different about him tonight, something in the way he looked at me, in the way he stood just inches away, as if he had been waiting for this moment for a long time.

Before I could say another word, Ayan leaned in and kissed me.

I froze for a second, caught completely off guard. But the moment his lips touched mine, every thought vanished. This was the moment I had unknowingly been waiting for—the one I had imagined but never dared to act on. His lips moved against mine, slow and gentle at first, as if testing the waters, but within seconds, the hesitation melted away. The kiss deepened, pulling me into a whirlwind of emotions I couldn't control.

Time ceased to exist. The world outside faded. All I could feel was him—his warmth, his touch, the way his hands firmly held my waist as if afraid to let go.

Ayan lifted me effortlessly and placed me on the hood of his car, never breaking the kiss. His lips trailed down to my neck, sending shivers through my body. My fingers curled into his shirt, holding onto him as if to steady myself.

I had never felt this way before. We kissed like we had been waiting for this forever. Like we were lost in each other and had finally found our way home.

When we finally pulled away, breathless and dazed, he cupped my face in his hands, his eyes locked onto mine. "I love you, Miraha," he said softly, his voice filled with certainty. For a moment, I just stared at him, trying to process his words. My heart raced.

He loved me?

A warm feeling filled me as I realized the truth. "I love you too," I said softly. Ayan smiled, his eyes glowing in the moonlight. He gently turned my face. "Look around," he said. I did, and gasped.

The whole place glowed under the soft light of the moon. The tall grass moved gently in the cold breeze, and I was surprised to see dozens of fireflies glowing around us, like tiny stars in the dark. It felt magical, like a dream. I had never seen anything so beautiful.

I stepped down from the bonnet, my feet touching the cool earth as I took in the breathtaking beauty of the moment. The fireflies flickered like tiny lanterns, and the wind carried the distant hum of the city, blending into the stillness around us.

As I stood there, lost in admiration, I felt Ayan's arms wrap around me from behind. His hold was firm yet gentle, his warmth pressing against me as he rested his chin lightly on my shoulder.

Neither of us spoke.

We didn't need words.

The silence between us was filled with something far greater—something raw and unspoken.

Then, I felt it.

A single tear landed on my shoulder.

I turned around, my heart tightening at the sight of Ayan's eyes glistening with emotion. He looked at me, his gaze filled with something so deep, so overwhelming, that I felt my breath hitch.

He cupped my face with both hands, pressing a soft kiss on my forehead.

"I love you," he whispered.

I had never been more sure of anything in my life. This was the man I wanted to grow old with.

I rose onto my tiptoes and kissed him, pouring every unspoken feeling into that moment. It was slow at first, tender and warm, but then it deepened, turning into something far more urgent. A war of emotions raged inside me, an undeniable pull I couldn't resist.

Ayan held me tightly, his arms securing me against him as if he never wanted to let go. The warmth between us intensified, the weight of our feelings pushing us closer, erasing every bit of distance. His fingers intertwined with mine, and without breaking the kiss, he gently led me to the back seat of the car.

There was no hesitation, no doubt. I felt his hands slide around my waist, pulling me onto his lap, his breath warm against my skin. My hands moved instinctively, unbuttoning the top of his shirt as I kissed him, wanting to feel him closer, wanting to lose myself in this moment.

But just as the heat of the moment took over, Ayan's hands caught mine, stopping me. His forehead rested against mine, our breaths mingling as he whispered, "Miraha, wait..."

I looked at him, my heart pounding, my emotions raw. I didn't want to stop. I had never felt this way before, not even with Rajiv. This was love, something deeper than anything I had ever known.

A Breath Away from Forever

Ayan's hands were still wrapped around me, his forehead resting gently against mine. I could feel his breath against my skin, warm and steady, as if he was trying to ground himself in this moment. He wanted me just as much as I wanted him. That much was clear.

But unlike me, he had the self-control to stop. I hated him for it.

I pulled back slightly, my frustration evident. He chuckled softly, brushing a strand of hair behind my ear. "I love the fact that you love me," he said, his voice warm yet firm. "And I'm happy that we finally showed our feelings to each other."

I sighed, still caught in the emotions of the moment. He pulled me into his arms again, holding me close, as if we had all the time in the world.

We stayed like that for a while, just breathing, feeling, existing in each other's warmth. After a long pause, I finally asked, "How did you find this place?" Ayan leaned back slightly, a small smile playing on his lips. "Some other time. I'll tell you later."

"No," I insisted, tilting my head to look at him. "I want to hear it now." He sighed in mock defeat, shaking his head. "Okay, okay," he said, running a hand through his hair. "After my breakup, I was at my lowest. I couldn't stay in my room. The walls felt like they were closing in on me. So one night, I just drove... aimlessly. No direction, no destination, just the road ahead. And somehow, I ended up here."

He glanced around, taking in the place like it still held pieces of those nights for him. "I kept coming back," he admitted. "I found peace here. I'd sit under the sky, watch the fireflies, and just... be."

His voice softened as he continued, "And after I met you, I knew I wanted to bring you here. I wanted you to see this place, to share this moment with you. But more than that, I was waiting for the right time... so I could confess my love under the moonlight and these fireflies."His eyes met mine again as he said, "I knew you would love it."

A warmth spread through my chest, and for a moment, I was speechless. "You were in love with me all this time?" I asked.

He smirked. "And planning all of this for weeks," he admitted. I blushed. "Didn't you feel it?" he asked, tilting his head. "The way I touched you? The way I played with your hair, the way I looked at you?"

I bit my lip, smiling. "I did," I confessed. "But I wasn't sure." He laughed softly, shaking his head before pulling me closer again.

Ayan's voice was soft and full of emotion as he spoke under the starry sky. "Miraha, the first time I saw you, when you stepped out of the car and our eyes met... my heart actually skipped a beat. You were so beautiful, standing there in the evening light. Your brown eyes completely captivated me. Since that day, I've been asking Suhana about you, dropping hints, and trying to organize get-togethers just to see you again."

As he spoke, I realized his feelings were just as deep as mine. It hit me—what I felt wasn't one-sided. It had been love at first sight for both of us.

The night grew darker, and the air turned cooler as fireflies danced around us. It was getting late, and even though we didn't want to leave, we knew it was time. With one last kiss, filled with the promise of tomorrow, we headed home—a night we'd always remember.

As soon as Ayan dropped me off, he called to check if I had made it inside safely. It was just another sign of his thoughtful nature that had been so clear since we first met.

Over the next few months, our love grew stronger. There was nothing better than being together. Eventually, I told Suhana about us. I had been nervous to share it with her, but her reaction was the most enthusiastic. "I knew it!" she exclaimed, hugging me tightly. "He's perfect for you!"

Ayan was everything I had hoped for and more. He pampered me in ways I had never experienced before. From the white roses he would surprise me with the unexpected dates and even picking me up from the airport after my long flights. Our touches, our kisses, our love, it was all intense and passionate.

I wanted to live in this bliss forever, but as is often the case, the universe seemed to have different plans for us. Monday morning started like any other, until I checked my emails.

The subject line read: **Transfer Approval – Mumbai Base.**

For a moment, my mind couldn't process what I was seeing. My fingers trembled as I clicked the email open, my eyes scanning the details. It was official. My transfer request had been approved. I had applied for it long before Ayan had come into my life, back when I had dreamed of moving closer to home. And then, somewhere along the way, I had completely forgotten to cancel it.

This should have been good news. I should have been happy. But I wasn't.

Instead, it felt like my heart was shattering into a million pieces. My breath became uneven, and before I knew it, tears welled up in my eyes. The thought of being away from Ayan was unbearable. Hyderabad and Mumbai weren't worlds apart, but a long-distance relationship? That had never been a part of my plan. And I was sure Ayan hadn't considered it either.

I knew I had to tell him. I couldn't delay this conversation. That evening, as always, Ayan and I had plans to meet. A drive and dinner, our usual escape from the world. But this time, it felt different. This time, I was carrying news that neither of us was ready for.

When he arrived to pick me up, I slid into the passenger seat, gripping my hands tightly in my lap. My mind was racing, trying to find the right words. But I couldn't speak. The silence stretched between us, thick and suffocating.

Ayan glanced at me, his brows knitting together in concern. "Did something happen on your flight?" he asked, his voice laced with worry. "Did someone say something to you?"

I looked at Ayan, my vision blurred with tears. The weight of the moment was unbearable. Every part of me wanted to hold on to him, to cling to this feeling, to pretend that none of this was happening.

Before I could stop myself, I threw my arms around him and broke down. My sobs came in waves, muffled against his chest as I finally let it all out. "Ayan... I got my transfer letter," I whispered through my tears. "I have to leave on the 20th." My voice cracked as I continued. "I tried everything... I tried to cancel it, to change it... but nothing can be done." His arms tightened around me, holding me as if he could keep me here just by the strength of his embrace.

For a long moment, he didn't say anything. knew what he was feeling because I felt it too—the sinking, gut-wrenching pain of knowing something was slipping away, and there was nothing we could do to stop it.

I pulled back slightly, looking up at him. His face was pale, his eyes glassy. "Ayan, I'm sorry..." I whispered. He cupped my face in his hands, his thumbs brushing away my tears. His own eyes were red-rimmed, his expression heavy with unspoken emotions.

"We knew this would happen sooner or later, right?" he said, his voice steady but heartbreakingly soft. I nodded, but the truth was, I had never actually prepared for this. "Twenty days," he murmured, more to himself than to me. "Eighteen, actually," he corrected with a small, sad smile. "That's how long we have left in Hyderabad."

I didn't want to think about it. Not now. "Then let's make these eighteen days unforgettable," I murmured, forcing a smile through my tears.

That night, we drove through the city like we always did, the silence between us filled with unspoken promises. We didn't talk about the goodbye that was coming; we just held onto the now. But I needed my people. I needed the gang. I texted the group, asking if they were free, and within minutes, plans were made.

Suhana was flying in that night, so we all decided to meet her at the airport. When we arrived, I spotted her the moment she walked out of the arrivals gate. Without thinking, I ran toward her and hugged her tightly.

The moment I broke down in her arms, she pulled back and looked at Ayan accusingly. "You idiot! What did you do?" she snapped, glaring at him. Ayan looked utterly confused. I shook my head, signaling her that it wasn't what she thought.

Her expression softened, concern replacing the frustration in her eyes. "What happened, Miraha?" she asked gently. And just like that, I broke down all over again.

We decided to sit at the food joint inside the airport, hoping that being together would make the weight of my news easier to bear.

Once everyone had settled, I took a deep breath, knowing I had to be the one to break the silence.

"I got my transfer to Mumbai," I said, my voice low but clear. For a moment, silence filled our table. Everyone seemed unsure of how to respond. Should they congratulate me or feel sorry that I was leaving? I couldn't blame them. I had been battling the same confusion since the moment I received that email.

Sean was the first to speak. He glanced at Ayan, then placed a reassuring hand on his shoulder before turning to the rest of the group. "We should be happy for her," he said, his tone light but deliberate. "She's going back to her family, right?" Ayan nodded, attempting a smile, but I could see right through it. It wasn't genuine. The usual warmth in his expression was missing, replaced by something else, something he was trying to hide.

The rest of the group still seemed hesitant, unsure of how to process the moment. The usual chatter, the effortless flow of conversation, felt forced. We ate in a strange mix of silence and small talk, each of us trying to pretend that this wasn't as big of a deal as it really was. But beneath the surface, the sadness was palpable.

When it was finally time to leave, Ayan and I walked back to his car in silence. The drive home was quiet, too quiet. Usually, the car would be filled with music, laughter, and our voices, but tonight, there was nothing. I wanted to say something, but I didn't know where to begin, and he didn't either. When we finally reached my building, I turned to him, waiting and hoping he would say something, but he just gave me a small nod.

"Goodnight," he said, his voice lower than usual. I nodded, feeling an ache in my chest as I stepped out of the car. That night, I kept checking my phone, waiting for his usual message, but it never came. For the first time since we started seeing each other, there was nothing from him—no "reached home?", no "goodnight," no "sweet dreams."

I tried to tell myself that he just needed time, that this was his way of processing things, but deep down, I knew what his silence meant. The next morning, my phone finally buzzed with a message from him: "I'm sorry about last night. I didn't mean to be distant. I really am happy for you. I just needed some time to process everything." I stared at the message, my fingers hovering over the screen.

He was trying to be strong, acting as though this wasn't breaking his heart just as much as it was breaking mine. But no matter how hard we pretended otherwise, we both knew this was going to change everything.

CHAPTER TEN

Goodbyes and New Skies

The coming week turned into a blur of flights and layovers, leaving me with hardly any time to catch my breath, let alone see Ayan. Our conversations were reduced to rushed texts between flights and late-night calls when I was too tired to think straight. I missed him. I missed all of them. But time was slipping through my fingers faster than I had expected.

Before I knew it, my departure was just a day away. On the evening of the 19th, Suhana called and insisted that I meet her and the others after I finished packing. Even if she hadn't asked, I knew I would have reached out to them. Saying goodbye to Hyderabad, to this life, without spending one last evening together was unthinkable. My flight was scheduled for the evening of the 20th, which meant I still had a little time.

After dinner at home and a final round of packing, I picked up my phone and called Ayan. "Pick me up at nine?" I asked, trying to keep my voice steady. "I'll be there before that," he said without hesitation. True to his word, he was outside my building by 8:45. As I stepped into the car, I took a deep breath, forcing myself to ignore the heaviness creeping into my chest.

Tonight wasn't about goodbyes. At least, that's what I told myself.

We were all meeting at Sean's place, and Ayan hadn't shared much about what was planned. I expected a casual gathering with some food, music, and the usual banter that always made time with them feel so effortless. But as soon as I stepped into Sean's flat, I froze.

The entire room was decorated with farewell balloons swaying from the ceiling. A table was loaded with a cake, pizza, chips, and drinks. As soon as I walked in, Raj and Kabir popped confetti into the air, filling the room with shimmering flares.

"Surprise!" they all shouted, their voices mixing with laughter and cheers. Kabir grinned and took my hand, pulling me into a playful dance as the others broke into an offbeat chorus, singing loudly and purposely out of tune. I laughed, letting the warmth of their love surround me. For a moment, I forgot about the clock ticking down. For a moment, I forgot I was leaving.

As Kabir twirled me around on the dance floor, he suddenly paused and glanced over at Ayan. A knowing smile spread across his face before he gently took my hand and led me toward him. Without a word, he placed my hand in Ayan's and gave me a reassuring nod.

The moment our fingers touched, my heart clenched. Our eyes met, and in that instant, everything around us faded. Neither of us spoke, but the weight of the moment hung between us. Tears brimmed in my eyes, mirroring the ones in his. Before I could say anything, Kabir suddenly pulled both of us into a tight hug. Within seconds, Raj, Sean, and Suhana joined in, wrapping us in warmth and laughter.

It was our first group hug. A bittersweet mix of sadness and joy filled the air. No words were needed; we all knew this was a moment we would carry with us long after I was gone.

"Alright, enough of this emotional drama," Kabir declared, breaking the silence. "It's our last party with Miraha. Let's make sure she remembers this night for all the right reasons, no more crying!" A chorus of agreements followed, and just like that, the energy shifted. I wiped my tears and smiled as they cheered me on. "Now, cut the cake already!" Sean said, pushing the knife into my hand. With everyone around me, their laughter filling the room, I took a deep breath and made the first slice.

The night stretched on as we lost ourselves in laughter, music, and conversations that we wished would never end. As I looked around, my heart swelled with gratitude. I turned to Suhana, knowing I had so much to thank her for.

"You know, I don't say this enough, but I really owe you," I said, my voice soft but full of meaning.

She raised an eyebrow, pretending not to understand. "For what exactly?" she teased.

"For coming into my life. For giving me this family away from home. For somehow being the reason Ayan and I found each other," I admitted, my voice thick with emotion.

A knowing smile crept onto her lips. "I'd love to take credit for that, but honestly, you two were bound to happen," she said with a wink.

I shook my head and pulled her into a tight hug. "Still, I'll always be grateful."

As much as I wanted to freeze this moment, reality had its own plans. Suhana's phone buzzed non-stop with calls from her mother, a reminder that it was late, and the night had to come to an end. We finally decided to wrap things up, even though none of us were ready to say goodbye.

One by one, I hugged everyone, holding onto them a little longer, knowing that while this wasn't the end of our friendship, it was the end of the way things had been. No more spontaneous meet-ups, no more aimless drives, no more lazy evenings spent doing nothing yet everything at once. Tomorrow, my company-arranged cab would take me to the airport, and with everyone caught up in their work schedules, there wouldn't be time for long farewells. This was it.

Ayan and I left Sean's place together, the silence between us saying more than words ever could. I stared out the window, watching the city blur past, my heart heavy with emotions I wasn't ready to confront. A few minutes passed before I realized something was off. The route was unfamiliar.

"Ayan... this isn't the way to my place," I said, glancing at him. He kept his eyes on the road but reached over to hold my hand. "Do you mind spending a little more time with me?"

"Not at all," I whispered, knowing that no amount of time would ever feel enough. As the car slowed, I recognized the place instantly. We had returned to the very spot where Ayan had first confessed his love to me.

As I stepped out of the car, the air was cool, carrying the faint scent of damp earth and wild grass. The sky was dark, not a full moon tonight, but the fireflies were still there, flickering like tiny stars floating just above the tall grass. Their soft glow cast a dreamy haze over the place, making everything feel almost unreal, like a scene from a forgotten dream.

I wrapped my arms around myself, feeling the weight of the moment settle in. This place had always been special, but tonight, it felt different—heavier, bittersweet. I turned to look at Ayan, and he was already watching me. His gaze held a thousand unspoken words, emotions swirling in his deep eyes.

Without thinking, I walked toward him, and he pulled me into a tight embrace. We held each other as if letting go would shatter something between us. I could feel his heartbeat against my chest, strong but uneven, just like mine. The ache inside me grew unbearable, and before I knew it, tears were rolling down my cheeks.

"I'm not ready to leave you," I whispered, my voice trembling.

Ayan's arms tightened around me. "I know," he said softly, his own voice breaking. "But you have to... and I have to let you go."

Tears streamed down both our faces as our lips met in a deep, lingering kiss—one filled with love, pain, and a silent promise.

When we finally pulled apart, he cupped my face in his hands and wiped my tears with his thumb. "I promise to love you forever, Miraha," he whispered. "You will always be in my heart... until we meet again."

I nodded, trying to smile through the tears, but my heart felt like it was breaking into a million pieces. We stood there for a while, just holding onto each other, memorizing every detail: the way our fingers intertwined, the warmth of his breath against my skin, the way his arms felt around me.

After what felt like forever, I took a deep breath and said, "Ayan, I don't want you to come to drop me tomorrow."

His expression changed instantly. "No, Miraha. I can't—" "It will be too hard," I interrupted gently. "I have a pickup arranged from my company, and I can't do this all over again. Please... promise me." He shook his head, unwilling to agree. "I don't think I can stay away, knowing you're leaving."

I took his hands in mine, squeezing them tightly. "Please, Ayan. For me. Let this be our goodbye." His jaw clenched, and after a long pause, he exhaled shakily. "Fine," he murmured. "But only because you're asking me to."

As we drove back to my PG, silence filled the space between us, except for the quiet sound of sniffles as we wiped away tears. When we reached, I turned to him one last time. "I love you," I said, my voice barely above a whisper.

Ayan pressed a soft kiss on my forehead. "I love you too, Miraha. Always." With a heavy heart, I stepped out, closing the door behind me. As the car pulled away, I felt my legs give out slightly, and I clutched my bag, willing myself not to break down. Tears fell freely as I made my way inside, but nothing could prepare me for the loneliness that settled in the moment I shut my door.

That night, we texted until our eyes couldn't stay open anymore. I don't remember when I finally fell asleep, but I know one thing: I woke up to a world that suddenly felt emptier without him.

As I left my building at 3 PM, the company car was already waiting. My bags were packed, and everything was in place, but my heart felt heavier with each passing second. I took a deep breath, stepped out of the building, and slid into the back seat. As the car pulled away, I turned my head, watching the familiar roads blur past, knowing that with every mile, I was leaving behind not just a city but a part of me that had belonged to Ayan.

My thoughts were loud, tangled between memories and the ache of separation. I had promised Ayan not to expect him at the airport, but as we approached the entrance, my eyes instinctively searched for him. I scanned every corner, every passing face, hoping that he had changed his mind, that he had come one last time. But he wasn't there.

I swallowed the lump in my throat and forced my feet forward. The airport doors slid open, and I stepped inside, feeling the weight of finality settle over me. The crowd moved around, travelers rushing past with their own stories, their own goodbyes, but I felt like I was moving in slow motion. I checked in, collected my boarding pass, and made my way to the gate. The waiting area was full, yet I felt alone. I stared at my phone, willing it to buzz, waiting for something, anything.

And then, it did. The screen lit up with Ayan's name. My breath hitched as I opened the message.

"I'll hold the memories of our time together always. I was a mess until I met you. I can't stop thinking about you, my heart is sinking without you. I won't be able to make it all alone without you. I pretended I was strong when I was hurt watching you go. No matter where you are, my love will continue to grow. Goodbye for now... until we meet again. Mine always."

My hands trembled as I read each word, my vision blurring with unshed tears. I wanted to reply, to tell him how much I loved him, how much I wished things were different, but no words felt enough. Instead, I pressed the phone against my chest, closing my eyes as a single tear rolled down my cheek. The final boarding call echoed through the terminal. It was time.

With a deep breath, I wiped my tears, picked up my bag, and walked toward the gate, carrying Ayan's words with me.

Tears rolled down my cheeks as I sank into my seat on the flight. As the plane climbed higher, I leaned against the window, watching the city lights fade into tiny specks before disappearing into the endless darkness below. The skyline I was leaving behind held so many memories, so many promises whispered in the dead of night.

I closed my eyes, trying to block out the ache in my chest. My head was throbbing, probably from all the crying and lack of sleep. I knew I needed rest, so I leaned back and let the soft hum of the plane calm me. Slowly, I drifted off.

The flight felt both endlessly long and short. Before I knew it, I was woken up by the sudden jolt of the landing. I blinked a few times, adjusting to my surroundings. Looking out of the window, I saw Mumbai. It felt familiar, yet something about it felt different this time. I should have been happy to be back home, but all I felt was an emptiness inside.

I grabbed my bags, made my way out of the airport, and took a cab home. The roads, the buildings, everything looked the same, yet I felt like a different person now. My heart raced as we neared my house. The moment

I stepped out of the cab, I saw my mom and brother waiting at the door, their faces lighting up the moment they saw me. I smiled for real this time. No matter what, being with them gave me a sense of comfort.

After settling in, I took out my phone and messaged Ayan and the rest of the gang. Reached home. Ayan replied almost immediately. Seeing his name on my screen made me realize more sharply that the distance between us was real now.

The next few weeks turned into a flurry of activity. Flying out of Mumbai was far more exhausting than anything I had experienced in Hyderabad. The sheer number of flights was overwhelming, and my schedule was packed to the limit. With our busy schedules, Ayan and I struggled to find time for each other, often relying on chats and video calls to stay connected despite the distance between us.

Every call was a mix of laughter and tears, as we shared stories about our days and how much we missed being together. We did our best to coordinate schedules and plan meetups whenever we could, but it often felt like fate was working against us. His demanding work as a car designer frequently clashed with my flying duties, leaving us both feeling frustrated and longing for each other's company.

Being a cabin crew member is no easy task, as it really takes a toll on your social life. While Ayan spent his weekends working on projects and eagerly waiting for any message from me, I was left hoping for his free time during my weekdays off. The distance was hard, but we never stopped being committed to each other.

Over the next few months, Ayan and I found ways to steal precious moments together, managing to meet once or twice a month despite our hectic schedules.Sometimes, I would fly to Hyderabad and stay with Suhana, stealing whatever time I could with Ayan. Other times, he would come to Mumbai, and we would book a hotel near my place, just so we could spend a few uninterrupted hours together. Those moments felt precious, like stolen time in a life that kept pulling us apart.

Long-distance was harder than we had imagined. No matter how much we loved each other, the gaps between our meetings stretched longer, and even our chats became less frequent. The effort to keep up with each other's lives started feeling exhausting, not because the love wasn't there, but because life kept getting in the way.

CHAPTER ELEVEN

At the Brink of Us

Soon it was October, and the month always had a way of making everything feel a little more nostalgic, a little heavier, as if change was just around the corner.

I was getting ready for my international flight from Mumbai to Muscat and back when my phone buzzed with a message from Ayan.

"I need to speak to you, are you free?"

I was in the middle of doing my makeup, carefully blending in the last touches. Without thinking much, I quickly replied, "BRB."

"OK," he responded almost instantly.

I didn't overthink it. He knew my flight schedule, and I figured whatever it was could wait until I was done. I finished my hair, threw on my uniform, and grabbed a quick dinner before rushing down to the cab that was already waiting for me outside. Sliding into the seat, I exhaled, finally settling into the rhythm of another workday.

As soon as I was in the car, I dialed Ayan's number. The call rang. No answer. I frowned but brushed it off, assuming he was caught up with something. I tried again. Still nothing. A small knot formed in my stomach, but I ignored it. I plugged in my earphones and turned up my music, letting the familiar playlist drown out my thoughts. The city lights streaked by as we made our way to the airport, the journey feeling routine, just like any other day.

At the airport office, I greeted my crew, and we huddled for the briefing. Our captain ran through the flight details while we nodded, taking in the usual safety checks and weather conditions. Once everything was cleared, we headed to the aircraft, going through the usual pre-flight procedures.

During any spare moments, I would steal a glance at my phone, hoping for any sign of a message from Ayan, but my screen remained disappointingly silent. Assigned to the aft section of the plane, which is the rear, I had a bit more flexibility to check my phone. Once boarding started, my mind switched into work mode. Passengers streamed in, some searching for their seats, others struggling with their luggage. I assisted where needed, helping an elderly man with his overhead bag and guiding a young mother with her baby. The usual chaos before takeoff kept me occupied.

When the doors were closed and the demo was completed, we prepared for takeoff. The familiar sounds of the aircraft filled the cabin, and as we soared into the sky, I knew that the next few hours would be packed with work. A three-and-a-half-hour flight to Muscat wasn't too long, but it was just enough time to complete the service, take a short break, and reset for the return leg.

Midway through the flight, after we had served meals and cleared the trays, I finally had a moment to breathe. I decided to make some tea for myself and the crew, hoping it would give me a bit of comfort. In the galley, one of my colleagues, Ananya, was busy with her own little creative experiment, melting chocolate over biscuits and trying to create some kind of makeshift dessert at 35,000 feet. We both laughed at the absurdity of it, the kind of small, silly moments that made long flights easier.

I leaned against the counter, stirring my tea, when my thoughts drifted back to my phone. Maybe Ayan had finally messaged. As I pulled out my phone, a strange uneasiness washed over me. My heart skipped a beat when I saw nine missed calls from Ayan. That was unlike him. He never called so many times unless something urgent had happened. With a growing sense of anxiety, I quickly checked my notifications. There was a message from him.

I opened it with shaky fingers.

"Mirahaa, where are you? I got a call from New York University for my car designing project. I have to leave next week! Where are you? I need to speak to you. Are you on a flight?"

For a moment, I just sat there, staring at the words on the screen, my mind struggling to process what I had just read.

Ayan was leaving.

New York. Next week.

A wave of emotions washed over me all at once—happiness, because this was his dream, but also fear and uncertainty. The thought of him being so far away made my chest tighten. Questions swirled in my mind: How would we make this work? How would we handle the time difference? What would this mean for us? Would things change?

I felt lightheaded, my breath uneven.

Ananya, who had been laughing with me just moments ago, must have noticed the change in my expression. She sat beside me, concern etched on her face. "Are you okay?" she asked gently.

I swallowed hard and nodded, but the truth was, I wasn't. I felt completely helpless. I wanted nothing more than to be back in Mumbai, to call Ayan, to hear his voice, to understand what this meant for our relationship. But I was stuck in the middle of an international flight with hours to go before I could do anything. I clenched my phone tightly, staring at the message, willing time to move faster. I needed to talk to him.

After touching down in Muscat, I kept checking my phone, reading Ayan's message over and over again. Each time, I hoped it would somehow change, that maybe I had misunderstood something, but the words remained the same. My heart felt heavier with each passing minute.

In the next fifty minutes, we were all set to board passengers for the flight back to Mumbai. It was getting harder for me to keep smiling, to greet passengers as they walked in. My emotions were pushing to the surface, and all I wanted to do was cry. But this was my job, and I had to hold it together.

Ananya, sensing that something was off, walked up to me and spoke softly. "You set up the food cart; I'll assist the passengers in the cabin," she said with a reassuring smile.

I nodded, feeling grateful for her kindness. I threw myself into work, keeping my hands busy so my mind wouldn't wander. The entire flight, I moved mechanically, setting trays, serving drinks, clearing up, but inside, I felt numb. I hardly spoke, barely smiled. It was a struggle to hold back the emotions that threatened to spill over at any moment.

After what felt like the longest flight of my life, we finally landed back in Mumbai. The moment we finished our post-flight duties, I rushed to the car parking lot. My hands were shaking as I got into the car and dialed Ayan's number. It was 7 AM. The phone rang.

He picked up almost immediately. "Hi," he said, his voice gentle. "I didn't know you had a flight, Miraha. I'm sorry..."

Sorry? Sorry?

I bit my lip, holding back the frustration building up inside me. Yes, he should be sorry—for leaving me here while he was about to fly off to New York. For making me feel like everything was slipping away. A hundred thoughts ran through my mind, but I couldn't say any of them.

Anger bubbled up inside me, and before I could stop myself, the words came out. "Okay! Congratulations, Ayan. That's big news. I'm happy for you," I said, my voice clipped and distant. "Can we talk later? I have a headache. Long flight, you know... Bye."

Before he could say anything, I hung up. My hands trembled as I switched off my phone. The moment the screen went black, the tears I had been holding back spilled over. I buried my face in my hands, my body shaking as silent sobs took over.

By the time I reached home, I felt emotionally drained. I walked straight to my room, barely making eye contact with my mom. "I'm exhausted," I mumbled. "Just need to sleep for a while."

She nodded, probably assuming it was just the exhaustion from my flight. I shut the door behind me, threw my bag onto the chair, and collapsed onto my bed.

Still clutching my pillow, I curled up, my face pressed into the fabric as I let the emotions take over. The pain, the confusion, the helplessness all hit me at once. I cried until my body couldn't take it anymore. Somewhere in between, exhaustion took over, and before I knew it, sleep pulled me under.

I finally stirred awake as the afternoon light slowly crept into my room. The warm glow stretched across the walls, painting faint patterns as it filtered through the curtains. It wasn't harsh or blinding, just warm enough to nudge me out of sleep. My head felt heavy, my body stiff from lying curled up for too long.

I reached for my phone, hesitating for a moment before switching it on. As soon as the screen lit up, a flood of notifications appeared, several missed calls and ten messages from Ayan.

"I'm sorry, Miraha. Please talk to me.

I didn't mean to upset you. I should have told you sooner.

Please don't be mad. I can't leave like this.

I love you, and I need you to understand."

One after another, his messages were filled with apologies, concern, and desperation. He wasn't trying to hurt me. He was just chasing the dream he had worked so hard for.

I sat by the window, staring at the world outside but not really seeing anything. My mind was racing with questions I had no answers to. What am I doing? Is this right? When I moved from Hyderabad, Ayan had been nothing but supportive. He never once made me feel guilty about leaving. He had never burdened me with his emotions, even when I knew it was hard for him. He had always been patient, always understanding. And now, when it was his turn to take a step forward, I was holding him back.

This was his dream. The opportunity he had been waiting for. The one he had spent years working towards. And here I was, making him feel guilty for it. I let out a shaky breath, feeling the weight of my own guilt pressing down on me. I'm the worst girlfriend ever. Without thinking twice, I picked up my phone and typed two simple words. I'm sorry. Not even a minute passed before my phone rang. It was Ayan. I swallowed hard, feeling an overwhelming sense of shame for how I had acted.

I took a deep breath and answered the call. "Hey, love..." Ayan's voice was soft, filled with hesitation. "I'm so sorry. I should have talked to you before accepting the offer. I was being selfish—"

"Stop," I cut him off gently. "Ayan, it's my fault. I overreacted. I know what this means to you, and I should have been happy for you instead of making it about us. I'm so, so sorry."

There was a pause, then his voice softened even more. "Miraha, stop saying sorry. I know what you're feeling. Who would understand better than me?"

That one sentence was enough to comfort me. I was still sad, but there was also relief. Ayan knew. He understood. He always did.

The rest of the month slipped away before I could fully grasp it. Ayan was buried in preparations, finalizing his visa, booking flights, arranging accommodation, and juggling the countless details that came with moving to a new country. Every time we spoke, he seemed caught between excitement and exhaustion, his mind constantly racing through things he had yet to do. I understood. I really did. But that didn't make missing him any easier.

I tried to push the thoughts away, to keep myself distracted with work and routine. But the truth lingered beneath everything. We were standing at the edge of a change neither of us could control. No matter how much we reassured each other, no matter how many times we said we'd make it work, reality was setting its own pace. And I was terrified of what that would mean for us.

November passed without us meeting each other. We lived through video calls, long messages, and stolen moments over the phone, stretching conversations late into the night just to feel close. But as much as I cherished them, they were never enough. The warmth of his presence, the comfort of knowing he was just a drive away, all of it was slipping further out of reach.

And despite everything, all I could do was watch time take him closer to his next chapter while I stayed behind, pretending not to feel the distance growing between us.

As the day of his departure got closer, Ayan made sure to stay in touch. Every free moment was filled with calls and messages, as if we were trying to hold onto every last second before he left. Even on the way to the airport, he kept texting, updating me on check-ins, security, and boarding. It felt like he was still right there, just a call away. But the moment his flight took off for New York, reality hit me harder than I expected.

That night, I kept checking my phone out of habit, even though I knew he'd be unreachable for at least 15 to 18 hours, factoring in the long journey and immigration. I tried to be patient, but the silence felt heavier than I imagined. A whole day passed. Then another. No calls. No messages. The absence of his presence started sinking in.

Just as I was beginning to spiral with worry, my phone rang. It was an unknown number. My heart skipped a beat as I hesitated before picking up.

"Hi, my love," came his familiar voice on the other end.

Relief washed over me instantly, and for the first time in two days, I let out a breath I didn't even realize I was holding.

CHAPTER TWELVE

The Parting Call

I had been waiting for this call, worrying nonstop, and now that he was finally here, I didn't know whether to yell at him or just listen.

"Where are you? Why didn't you call me sooner? Do you even know how worried I was?" I fired my questions one after the other, unable to hold back.

Ayan chuckled on the other end, his voice warm and familiar. "Love, relax. I'm here. I love you."

I took a deep breath, feeling some of the tension leave my body. "I love you too," I muttered, finally letting myself settle into the moment.

For the next half an hour, he spoke nonstop. He told me about his new place, how cold it was in New York, how different everything felt. I listened, holding onto every word, feeling like I was right there with him. Even with the miles between us, his voice had a way of making me feel close.

"Love, I just reached my institute," he said eventually. "I'll call you tonight, okay?"

"Okay," I whispered, not wanting to let go just yet.

He kissed me over the phone, and just like that, the call ended.

The next few weeks were a flurry of time differences and busy schedules. Ayan was drowning in work, settling into his routine, while I was constantly on flights. We tried to stay connected with quick chats and stolen moments between meetings and layovers. At times, our conversations turned into teasing, playful messages about how much he missed kissing me, how he could still remember the taste of my lips. It was our way of holding on. But no matter how hard we tried, the distance was beginning to feel real.

December arrived, bringing the holiday season in full swing. Ayan would send me pictures of Christmas decorations in New York, the lights, the snow, the celebrations. Meanwhile, I kept up with him on social media, scrolling through posts of him spending time with his colleagues, making the most of his new life. He was busy, I was busy, and gradually, without even realizing it, our worlds began to drift apart.

Then, the cracks slowly began to appear. No matter how much two people love each other, sometimes love alone isn't enough.

At first, it was small things: missed calls, delayed replies, half-hearted conversations. But soon, those little things started turning into fights. The frustration of not being able to see each other, the exhaustion from long days, and the weight of our own separate lives started pressing down on us.

"You don't even try anymore, Ayan," I snapped one night when he finally called after three days of silence.

His voice was laced with exhaustion. "Miraha, it's not like that. I barely get time to sleep, let alone sit on calls for hours. You know that."

"I don't need hours! I just need you to at least talk to me properly when we do get time."

"I do! But you're always complaining! Every call turns into a fight. Can't we just talk like we used to?"

I let out a frustrated sigh. "How can I talk when you barely sound like you want to? It's like I'm forcing you to be here." His silence on the other end felt heavier than any words.

Soon, the calls became shorter and the chats became less frequent. Mornings and goodnights were the only messages we exchanged most days. At one point, we used to share every little detail of our day, but now, there were things left unsaid, updates that never got shared. Days passed where we didn't talk at all, and the worst part was, neither of us fought to fix it anymore.

It wasn't his fault. It wasn't mine either. Maybe, deep down, we both knew we were holding on to something we had already started losing.

Ayan, being the gentleman I knew him to be, never had the heart to admit how burdensome our relationship had become. It was January 30th when I finally mustered the courage to address what had been weighing on us both. That day, I had asked him to set aside some time because I needed to talk. Not through a rushed voice note. I needed to see and hear him.

"Hey Ayan, how are you?" I started, trying to keep my tone light.

"Good," he responded, but his image on the screen looked strained, and his voice lacked its usual warmth.

We spoke normally for a bit, about his classes, my flights, the usual. But I couldn't keep avoiding it. I took a deep breath and finally said what had been on my mind for weeks.

"Ayan, I love you, and I don't doubt that for a second, but this distance... It's tearing me apart. It's affecting our mental peace. I think you feel the same, don't you? Please, I need to hear your thoughts."

There was a heavy pause on the line, a silence that spoke volumes. Finally, Ayan spoke, his voice heavy with emotion.

"Miraha... I feel the same."

The moment he said my name, my heart cracked. In all these years, he had never called me that. It had always been "love." No matter how much we argued, no matter how upset we were, it had always been "love."

My throat tightened, my chest ached. Isn't this what I wanted? I told myself this was the right thing to do, that this was for the best. Then why did it feel like my whole world was caving in? I swallowed hard, forcing myself to stay strong, to hold back the tears threatening to spill.

Ayan continued gently, "Miraha, I know you're strong. And everything you're saying... it's true. If we look at where we are, the situation we're in, this is the right thing to do." He took a deep breath. "But I love you. I always will. And this time, I want to agree with you—to let you go."

Hearing those words shattered me. My hands shook as I looked at his pixelated face, the faint glow of the screen reflecting in his eyes. He seemed so distant, almost unreachable. I tried to hold myself together, swallowing the lump in my throat, but then I heard it, his quiet, broken sobs crackling through the speakers. That was it. I broke down too.

We weren't just ending a relationship; we were letting go of something that had been so rare, so beautiful—something neither of us could ever replace.

"I don't know what life has in store for us, but let's hope our paths cross again someday," Ayan said softly, and I could see the pain in his eyes through the screen.

I could see him fumbling with something on his screen. Suddenly, the haunting notes of "Take My Breath Away" from Top Gun filled the silence between us. It was our song, a reminder of how it all started, and now, it seemed, how it was ending.

I wiped my tears, forcing a small smile. "Take care, Ayan. I wish you all the best on this journey. You've worked so hard to get where you are, and I know you'll go even further. I'm sure our paths will cross again someday. Until then... it's goodbye."

The song played in the background, its melody bittersweet, underscoring the surreal feeling of our parting. For a moment, it felt like we were both holding on to something we weren't ready to let go of. "I will always love you, Miraha," he managed to say, his voice breaking.

"I love you too," I whispered back, the words heavy with all the love and pain of our parting. Those were the last words we shared before the call disconnected, the song still playing as the screen went black, leaving me in the quiet of a room too big for one.

I spent the entire night crying, my heart heavy with the knowledge that Ayan was likely doing the same, despite the miles between us. The days that followed were some of the hardest I had ever faced. Every time my phone rang, I hoped it was him, but it never was. I knew I had to accept the reality of our situation, but my heart fiercely resisted. Tears became a daily part of my life; every little thing seemed to remind me of him.

Then, on February 14th, a package arrived for me. My hands trembled as I read the sender's name. Ayan.

Inside, there was a box of chocolates, an artificial red rose, and a folded letter. My eyes welled up as I held them close. I clutched the package, ran into my room, and locked the door behind me. As I sat on my bed, staring at the unopened letter, I realized that some love stories don't end. They just find a different way to exist.

With shaky hands, I finally unfolded the letter, bracing for the wave of emotions I knew it would bring. Ayan's handwriting brought an immediate sense of closeness, despite the physical distance between us. His words flowed effortlessly:

"To my love,

Our love story remains unfinished, but the memories we've created will forever reside within me. You've made me a better person, and for that, I am eternally grateful. I will always cherish every moment spent with you, holding a special place in my heart. And just as you hoped, I too wish that our paths might cross again someday. Yours always..."

A tear rolled down my cheek as I read the words that felt like they were pulled straight from my own mind. I smiled through the tears, moved by the lasting mark his love had left on my heart.

Even though he wasn't here, I could still feel him all around me, like a comforting hug. With a deep sigh, I set the letter down next to the rose, a reminder of our unending love, and softly said, "Till we meet again, my love."

That night, I sat in my room, staring at the letter, its edges fluttering slightly in the breeze from the open window. The box of chocolates remained untouched beside it, a silent witness to the emotions swirling inside me. My mind drifted between the past and the present, torn between holding on and letting go.

Then, my phone rang, snapping me out of my thoughts. The number was unfamiliar. Hesitating for a second, I picked up.

"Hi, Miraha." It was a woman's voice.

"Hello? Who is this?" I asked, confused.

"This is Chhavi... Rajiv's friend."

My stomach tightened at the mention of his name. Of all nights, why did this have to happen now? I wanted to hang up immediately, but Chhavi hadn't done anything wrong. I decided to hear her out.

"Yes? What is it?" I said, keeping my tone neutral.

"Miraha, Rajiv told me everything... about what happened between you two, about the way he behaved. He's really sorry. He's not doing well, and he just wants to talk to you. Please, just once... for me."

A part of me screamed no. I owed him nothing. But another part of me, the one that had known heartbreak all too well, understood what it felt like to lose someone you once loved. I let out a slow breath.

"Fine," I said. "I'll talk to him."

There was silence for a second before I heard his voice.

"Hi, Miraha..."

I closed my eyes, steadying myself. "Hmm," I responded, my voice unreadable. "Tell me."

A conversation I never thought I'd have was about to begin.

Rajiv's voice was softer than I had ever heard it before. There was no arrogance or anger, just remorse. "I'm ashamed of how I treated you, Miraha," he said. "I realize now that my behavior was unacceptable. It wasn't your fault for running away from me. Any girl would have done the same after what I put you through."

There was a pause. I could hear him take a shaky breath before continuing.

"I'm not calling to ask for anything. I don't expect us to be friends or to undo the past. I just need to ask for your forgiveness... for closure."

For the first time, Rajiv sounded genuinely sorry. His words didn't feel rehearsed or forced. They came from a place of regret, and I could sense the weight he carried. "I forgive you, Rajiv," I said after a moment. "And... if I ever hurt you in any way, I'm sorry too."

"You didn't," he replied. "Thank you, Miraha. I mean it. I wish you all the best for the future. Take care."

"Take care too, Rajiv. Bye," I said, ending the call. I sat back, a mix of emotions swirling within me.

I stared at my phone, processing everything. It felt surreal. In a single day, two chapters of my life had closed, one filled with love and the other with pain. And as I sat there in silence, I realized that sometimes closure doesn't come with answers. It comes with acceptance.

Epilogue

As I finished narrating my story, my emotions felt raw, as if I had relived every moment, every rush of excitement, every heartbreak, every silent ache that had settled deep within me. I exhaled slowly, looking up at Nina and Ayushi, who sat across from me, completely engrossed. Their eyes held the weight of everything I had just shared.

For a moment, none of us spoke. The air was thick with reflection, the kind that settles in after hearing something real, something unfiltered.

"And then, a couple of months later, I got selected here, and the three of us met again," I finally said, my voice lighter now, bringing the story full circle. "Now we're not just friends. We're roommates, sisters... like family away from home."

Nina leaned in, her expression unreadable, but her eyes held a glimmer of something—maybe curiosity, maybe admiration. Ayushi, on the other hand, tried to mask the sympathy she felt, lighting another cigarette as if to shake off the emotions lingering in the room.

I stretched my arms and let out a tired sigh. "Alright, enough of my emotional roller-coaster. It's almost five in the morning. We need to sleep, we have grocery shopping to do tomorrow."

"Shut up, Miraha," Ayushi said suddenly, wrapping her arms around me. Within seconds, Nina jumped in between us for a tight group hug, making it impossible to breathe but filling the moment with warmth.

"Coffee, anyone?" Nina asked, breaking the silence.

"Yes, please!" Ayushi and I said in unison, raising our hands without hesitation.

Nina got up and stretched, walking toward the kitchen. "Alright, coffee coming up!" she announced, tying her hair up into a loose bun. Ayushi leaned back on the couch, letting out a long sigh as she stared at the ceiling. "I swear, Miraha, your love life is quite something," she said, exhaling smoke from her cigarette. "Ayan, Rajiv, the drama, the passion, the heartbreak, it's got everything." She shook her head and gave me a teasing smirk.

I laughed, shaking my head. "You both have your own stories too, don't act like mine is the only one worth telling." I glanced at Ayushi knowingly. "You and Rohan... still going through the same cycle?"

She scoffed, tapping her cigarette against the ashtray. "What do you think? He messes up, I scream, he apologizes, and I forgive him. Then repeat."

Nina placed three cups of coffee on the table and sat down with a sigh. "You know what I envy about your story, Miraha?" she said, wrapping her hands around her cup. "You and Ayan... even though it didn't work out, it was real. You let each other go with love, not hate. No unfinished business, no grudges. It was just pure."

I nodded, stirring my coffee. "But you and Vikram have something solid too. You've been together for years."

She let out a small chuckle. "Yeah, but long-distance is no joke. He's stationed miles away, and sometimes I feel like I'm in a relationship with my phone instead of him. But then he comes back, and it's like none of that ever mattered." She paused, taking a sip. "I guess every love story has its complications."

I looked at the two of them, my heart full. We were three very different women, yet somehow, our lives had woven into each other's in ways that felt irreplaceable.

I leaned back into the couch, my body sinking into its familiar comfort as my gaze wandered toward the window. Faint streaks of pink and orange began to creep across the horizon, transforming the quiet stillness of the sky into a soft, glowing dawn.

As I watched this unfold, it struck me how much life mirrors the sky. Just as night transitions into day and back again, life reveals itself in cycles, each with its own shades and lessons. Love, I thought, is much the same. It comes in so many shades, each unique in its depth and meaning. There's the warmth of love that fills you with a sense of belonging, the ache of love that leaves you raw and vulnerable, and the fleeting moments of love that pass through your life like whispers carried by the wind.

Each chapter of love I've experienced has its own story, its own purpose. Some taught me to open my heart. Others reminded me of the resilience that comes from healing. And even the fleeting ones, the loves that came and went too quickly, left mc with lessons I didn't know I needed.

Who knew what stories were yet to be told?